求職英語一本通

一本通

適合各行各業的面試實戰指南

Zephyr Yeung 著

U0099855

萬里機構

年輕人初出茅廬是充滿了迷茫的，如果得到一本好的書本扶助，足以能夠贏在起步，改變他的人生！

我輩已年長老大了，在這個時候最關心的就是如何將經驗和實踐所得傳承下一代，而 Zephyr 正是我們期待和追求的新一代成長模式。她正面、樂觀、勤力奮鬥，是年青新一代的楷模，她不單學有所成，到了今日更加已為人師表去培育新一代！這年青語言學家正在語言科學上研究，為將來的社會作出更大的改變，她的成就令我這個長輩實在非常羨慕她的父母！

Zephyr 的翻譯水平專業精簡有力。我是香港的樓市評論員，就市場新常態要發表新的市場理論，一些理論是需要著書立說甚至要在西方市場發表的，在翻譯上因新經濟沒有先例的關係極具挑戰，其中「龍市理論（Dragon Market）」就是一個好例子，Zephyr 為我將其中理論的基礎結構作翻譯，非常清晰明瞭，令我的市場理念可以與歐美的朋友分享，我十分讚賞。

我在公職上亦在僱員再培訓局工作了 6 年，除了是董事局成員之外，我有 5 年時間是「課程及服務發展委員會」召集人，主持課程審批工作，在工作中我感到偉大的時代正衝擊着香港新一代！但這並非不幸，不斷的「變」會帶來大量的新機會！年輕人要加油！這本書我認為是象徵了香港新一代的真正精英！希望讀者可以一起追隨 Zephyr，一起走上時代的高速公路！

汪敦敬

榮譽勳章（MH）
僱員再培訓局委員（2012-2018）
僱員再培訓局「課程及服務發展委員會」召集人（2013-2018）
地產代理監管局委員（2014-2020）

「知識上的投資」也可得到很好的回報，這本書正好給我一個很好的答案，要有好的語言和文字根底，才可洞悉和掌握社會上的機會。

我看着 Zephyr 長大，別家的孩子嘻嘻哈哈地在玩耍，她卻只愛看書，不論任何文字的書籍也都喜愛，這就種下她深厚的語文根基。

Zephyr 了解年青人對語文的困難，用嶄新的方式教導學生，簡單清楚亦容易明白，今次破天荒出書，把難於理解的英文，重點地化繁為簡地解釋，使讀者輕鬆地增值知識，說句老實話，知識增值比投資增值更重要！

陳菜菁博士

FMBA, C. Mgr, D. Mgt.
祥益地產代理有限公司行政總裁
林肯大學榮譽管理博士
加拿大特許管理學院院士

自序

基於各種各樣的不利因素，本港經濟近年持續低迷、失業率一直高企。突如其來的疫症，成為壓垮駱駝的最後一根稻草，眾多行業不勝負荷，翻起一浪接一浪大規模的裁員潮和倒閉潮，不少市民不幸受到波及，深陷失業停工的彷徨當中。就業市場趨於黯淡，要在此時此地覓得一份心儀的工作，實在談何容易呢。

競爭激烈的求職市場就仿如一個槍林彈雨的戰場，一步一驚心。常言道「機會只會留給有準備的人」，在求職道路上，立心克服挑戰、逆境前行的你，理應及早好好裝備自己，才有機會克敵制勝，打一場漂亮的勝仗。不少人以為求職不外乎就是「投寄求職信和履歷表、面試、等候通知」而已，然而，求職一事又豈止於此？求職市場上人浮於事，想突圍而出，箇中大有學問。

因此，筆者特意編寫了這一本協助求職者順利踏入職場的書。**本書依照求職到入職的先後順序進行編排設計，從求職時如何撰寫求職信、履歷表、回覆面試通知、面試、面試後續（除了要學會如何應對面試外，求職者也要學會如何於面試結束的後續工作等方面做得面面俱到），到初進公司的實用日常對答，**統統一應俱全，協助求職者一步一步為邁進職場做好準備。

你試過頻頻投寄 C.V.（履歷表）和求職信卻總等不到回音嗎？你可能以為是因為自己的資歷不夠優秀，所以未能取得面試機會。但是，你可曾想過這其實和你撰寫 C.V. 和求職信的技巧有關係？你又試過因面試失敗而與心儀職位擦肩而過嗎？又或，面試表現「自我感覺良好」，但面試後經歷漫長的等待，結果原來再次「食白果（白忙一場、毫無收穫）」嗎？

面試失敗難道是因為運氣不夠好嗎？與其怨天尤人，不如想想自己到底有沒有在面試前做好準備工夫。現今社會，學歷和工作經驗已經不再是企業選賢的唯一考慮因素，求職者於面試的表現同樣備受重視。毫無疑問，面試早已成為求職者進入心儀公司的必經之路，再加上社會競爭愈演愈烈，面試已經發展成為一種專業性的測試。

面試過程中的每個環節、每道問題都是決定面試是否成功的關鍵。成功非僥倖，能否於面試中脫穎而出取決於個人的努力和準備。在考試中，學生要做足準備才能取得佳績；在比賽中，選手要準備好才能有信心打敗對手；在面試中，面試者也應事先做好準備才可穩操勝算。面試講求臨場發揮，沒有十拿九穩之說，假如你是一名社會新鮮人，本身已經缺乏經驗，再加上準備不足的話，分分鐘機會來到你面前，你想接都接不住，最終白白讓機會溜走。

自以為已為面試做好準備的你，真的掌握好面試的技巧和訣竅了嗎？問問自己，你有沒有嘗試在面試中打動面試官？你有沒有在面試接近尾聲時作出最後一擊，向面試官提出有建設性的問題？如果沒有的話，就說明你還未 ready 打這一仗，還需多加學習和鍛煉。

你希望得到更多的面試機會嗎？你希望在面試官心目中留下更好的印象嗎？你希望在面試中獲得面試官的青睞嗎？想要學會如何完美地避開面試的「地雷」、精確地拿出適用的「殺手鐧」嗎？那麼，你便需要細閱這本書，學習一下相關技巧了。

本書分為三大部分：Part 1 針對求職相關的問題，包括如何撰寫讓僱主眼前一亮的「求職信」和「履歷表」、如何在電郵和電話回覆 face-to-face 和 video（視像）面試通知、如何於面試後撰寫 thank-you letter（感謝函），以及這一章節的主角之一 ——「熱門面試問題」。在這部分，編者精心為你網羅了 job interview 中各種熱門的問題，並附上必學技巧、實用句型及詞彙、對答範例等，當中還包括了近年流行的 Video interview（視像面試）的小貼士。

Part 2 包含了熱門職位（包括：市場營銷、餐飲業、接待員、秘書、辦公室文員 / 白領、地產 / 保險經紀和銷售員等）的 interview 真實演練，帶你還原面試現場，與你一起提前體驗面試的過程。

最後，附錄部分提供了「初入公司」的注意事項、對答範例、必學詞彙等等。這部分包括了不同情景的對答範例，例如「上班第一天」、「結識新同事」、「向新老闆 / 上司介紹自己」、「熟悉工作環境」等，可謂應有盡有。

除此之外，亦提供了針對辭職相關的事宜，例如在職期間如何請假去面試、如何撰寫得體的「辭職信」、被公司挽留應如何應對、如何爭取加薪等等。

閱讀本書時，你也可以掃描出現在對答範例旁邊的 QR code 來聽聽說話者說話的語調、語速和發音，並嘗試自己跟著唸一次。這個部分只要多加練習，應用時就能從容不迫、得心應手，把自己最好的一面呈現出來。

總括而言，**本書是特別為職場新鮮人以及重回職場的求職者而設的踏腳石，並在激烈的求職競賽中穩中求勝。**編者盡力將書中每一部分都做到深入淺出且簡明扼要，方便廣大讀者學習。

最後，衷心祝願大家都能在職場上，成為一名真正的「職場英語達人」！

～祝大家在求職路上順順利利、馬到功成！～

Zephyr

2021 年 4 月

求職英語一本通

6

目錄

Part 1

求職相關的問題

Chapter 01 撰寫求職信

Chapter 02 撰寫履歷表

Part 2
熱門職位真實演練

Appendix 1

初入新公司

Appendix 2

辭職相關事項

Part 1

求職
相關的問題

「求職信」顧名思義就是以應徵工作為由而書寫的信件，不同人士都有機會需要撰寫求職信，然而，撰寫求職信的目的只有一個 —— 讓招聘者或是僱主給予自己面試、甚至入職的機會。筆者曾經聽過不少人將求職信比喻為打開職場新一頁的一把鑰匙，細想起來，這比喻還果真是頗貼切的。

大多時候，招聘者與應徵者在正式面試前都是素未謀面的，招聘方需要在成千上萬的應徵申請中挑選出合適的人選實在不容易，可以用作考慮的資料不多，而求職信正好就是其中的一大憑藉。顯然易見，求職信是求職者向招聘者好好介紹自己不可或缺的一大工具，亦是向對方展示自己的第一步。好的求職信不但能夠讓對方對自己的背景有更深入、透徹的了解，更能達到推銷自己的目的，給對方留下深刻印象，進而贏得面試機會。由此可見，求職信對於求職者而言相當重要，甚至有可能在求職一事上成為成敗的關鍵之一。

學會撰寫求職信固然是必須的，而學會撰寫一封專業得體的求職信也是相當重要。剛畢業的職場「新鮮人」也許會因為缺乏撰寫求職信的經驗，而未必能寫出一封合格的求

職信。然而，你是否真的有把握撰寫出一封大方體面而又抓住招聘者注目的求職信呢？要學習撰寫一封好的求職信，首先我們要了解一下求職信的基本結構。

求職信（Cover Letter）的基本結構如下：

NEW MESSAGE

Part 1 電郵主旨 Subject Line

Sent to ▓▓▓▓▓▓▓▓

Part 2 上款 / 稱謂 Opening Salutation

Part 3 開場白 / 引言 Introductory Paragraph

Part 4 正文 Body Paragraphs

Part 5 結束語 Closing Statement

Part 6 下款 / 結尾敬語 Closing Salutation

Send

求職相關的問題

1.1 電郵主旨

說起撰寫求職信，不少人都會側重於構思內容，一心以為只要施盡渾身解數，把求職信如雕花般雕琢出來，把內容修改得盡善盡美、完美無瑕，那就可以成功取得對方的注視，最終定能得到別人的認同並獲得寶貴的面試機會。注重求職信內容本身並無不妥，但這類人總因為過於着重內容而忽略了周邊的細節，因而白白浪費了一封花了不少心血換來的求職信，同時也斷送了一個向對方推銷自己的大好機會。

在撰寫求職信這事上，過往側重於「雕琢」內容的你，可曾想過電郵主旨（Subject Line）的重要性？你又可曾為擬定電郵主旨花過心思？無論求職信的內容撰寫得怎麼無懈可擊、怎麼引人入勝，如果 Subject Line 沒好好寫的話，很容易給對方留下一個不良的印象，最終背上「馬虎」、「不專業」、「沒新意」等等的「污名」。

再者，一間企業或公司每天都需要處理成千上萬的電郵，Subject Line「貌似不重要」的電郵很容易會被忽略，甚至被看漏眼。如果你把求職電郵的 Subject Line 草草了事的話，這分分鐘導致你那完美的求職信「石沉大海」。

所以作為求職者的你，就算已手持一封完美的求職信，也絕不能鬆懈，必須花點心思和時間，認真學習一下如何擬定一個醒目的 Subject Line，用有限的字數讓自己的求職電郵突圍而出。

Subject Line 應該寫多長？

每封電郵主旨大約能顯示 60-70 個字符（e.g. "application" 有 11 個字符）。換言之，長度大概在 6 至 10 個英文字為理想，請保持信件主旨簡短而清晰具體。

小貼士

1. 由於信件主旨（Subject Line）是你給對方的第一印象，因此，在發送電子郵件前，請確保信件主旨清晰且沒有錯誤。

2. 單刀直入，把重點放在最前。例如：申請職位（Position）。

3. 主旨中宜加入 "Job Application"、"Ref. no（職位參考編號）" 等字眼。

供「社會新鮮人」參考的主旨示例

- Job Application: Sandy Chan for Marketing Assistant (Ref: 1234)

- Re: Application for Sales Associate (#325178)

- Junior Software Engineer Seeks Software Developer Position (Ref: 954)

- Application for Personal Assistant （#145615）

- Job Application: Chelsea Choi for Management Trainee (#9839)

- Re: Application for the position of Project Coordinator

供「已經有一定經驗的職場老手」參考的示例（*可在 Subject Line 提及「工作年資」，使其更引人注目。）

📌 Office Manager with 10 Years of Experience

📌 Senior Software Engineer - 10+ Years' Experience

供由某人推薦參考的示例（*可在 Subject Line 提及「推薦人的名字」，以引起收件人的注意。）

📌 Referred by David Wong - Engineer Role

📌 Referred by Zephyr Yeung for Teaching Assistant

1.2 上款 / 稱謂

"Dear"

⬇

+ 對方的尊稱（Honorific Title）

Mr（先生）	**Mrs**（夫人）	**Miss**（小姐）	**Ms**（女士）	**Dr**（博士）

⬇

+ Surname（姓氏）

例子：

假如你知道收件人的名字

📌 Dear Mr Chan,

📌 Dear Dr Yeung,

📌 Dear Miss Wong,

📌 Dear Ms Choi,

假如你不知道收件人的名字
（*要盡可能詢問到對方的商務頭銜）

📌 Dear Hiring Manager（招聘經理），

📌 Dear Human Resources Manager（人力資源部經理），

📌 Dear Recruitment Manager（招聘經理），

假如你不知道收件人的名字和商務頭銜

📌 Dear Sir / Madam,

小貼士

1 撰寫求職信前，先花點時間找找收件人的名字以表誠意。若實在無法得知收件人的名字，也要盡力找出對方的頭銜。假如你真的找不到相關資料，才用 "Dear Sir / Madam" 作為為上款吧！

2 切忌稱呼對方的全名

✗ Dear Mr Peter Chan,

✓ Dear Mr Chan,

3 為為了維持專業形象，切忌使用看起來不專業或不成熟的電郵地址

✗ sweety123@email.com

✗ adorable_me_1998@email.com

✗ prettycherryLOL@email.com

✓ peter.chan@email.com

✓ kurtyeung@email.com

✓ sychan@email.com

"My name is xxx. I am writing to apply for the position of..."

這是你平常撰寫求職信會寫的開場白嗎？這種求職信的開場白相當常見，HR 閱人無數，每天過目的求職信多不勝數，面對千篇一律、平淡無奇的開場白，確實得難以提得起勁，亦令你的求職信難以在眾多求職者中突圍而出。

求職信的第一個段落，往往就是開場白，亦即是引言的部分。一個別出心裁的開場白有利於勾起 HR 繼續閱讀下去的意欲，説不定還能打響頭炮，為求職者的形象加分，並在 HR 心目中建立一個美好的印象。有沒有想過為甚麼自己一次又一次寄出求職信，千盼萬盼卻總盼不到回音？其中一個可能就是因為你的求職信欠缺一個與眾不同、能取得對方注意的開場白，讓你「輸在起跑線上」，最終落得失敗收場。

不想再重蹈覆轍嗎？首先，你需要學會撰寫吸睛的開首方式，在黃金 7 秒內抓住 HR 的注目，繼而吸引對方耐心閱畢你辛辛苦苦寫的求職信。記着，一封好的求職信是逆轉勝的關鍵，一個好的求職信開場白是求職路上取勝的第一步！

七種求職信的開首方式

1 表達對公司的熱情
Convey enthusiasm for the company

2 凸顯與彼方公司的關連
Highlight a mutual connection

3 提出目標公司具新聞價值的時事
Bring up something newsworthy

4 描述令人矚目的成就
Tailor accomplishments to your cover letter

5 表達自己對工作的熱情
Express your passion & excitement

6 說一個引人入勝的故事
Tell a creative story

7 簡單描述自己
Start with a belief statement

求職相關的問題

假如你本來已經是該公司的顧客，甚至是忠實客戶，那麼，這面試將會是一個很好的機會，讓對方感受你對他們公司的商品或服務的熱情。然而，表達自己的情感時切忌過分浮誇，否則，對方會認為你太虛偽的。

Useful words & expressions

to drive growth (v phr.)	推動增長；促進增長
high-traffic events (n phr.)	高流量活動
a product launch party (n phr.)	產品發佈會
a great fit for the role (n phr.)	非常適合擔任該職位
new arrivals (n phr.)	剛上架的新品
reputation (n.)	名譽
well-known (adj.)	知名的；出色的
to combine my interests with this position (v phr.)	把我的興趣和這個職位結合起來
I would be well suited to the position because_____	我很適合這個職位，因為 _____
My area of expertise is_____	我的專業領域是 _____

求職信開場白範例

"Since I first discovered 3+3 Collection, I have been a big fan of your company and the products you offer. I was excited to see that 3+3 Collection is hiring **an Event Coordinator**（活動協調員）who is skilled at selecting venues, arranging event services, and **driving growth**（推動增長）with **high-traffic events**（高流量活動）- especially since I've attended a number of your company's **in-store events**（店內活動）, such as **charity events**（慈善活動）, holiday events, and 2020's **product launch party**（產品發佈會）. With my three-year background in organizing events with **a blend of technology**（各種技術）in the **corporate**（企業的；職場的）space, I believe that I am **a great fit for the role**（非常適合擔任該職位）."

② 凸顯與彼方公司的關連

如果是你經某人（e.g. 舊同事、在你申請的公司工作的朋友）轉介你應徵這份工作的話，求職信的開首可以考慮略略提及該推薦人 / 轉介人。

to reach out to you (v phr.)	與您聯繫
to refer (v.)	推薦
to coordinate (v.)	協調
to cooperate (v.)	合作
my former colleague (n phr.)	前同事
to work closely together (v phr.)	密切合作
to analyze (v.)	分析
to implement (v.)	實施
strategic (adj.)	有助於計劃成功的；戰略（性）的
to expand company's customer base (v phr.)	擴大公司的客戶群
to build long-lasting customer relationships (v phr.)	建立長期的客戶關係
a good match for this position (n phr.)	很適合這個職位

> **範例**

求職信開場白範例

"I was excited to learn of this job opportunity from my former colleague Cherry Lam. Cherry suggested I **reach out**（與……聯繫）to you regarding the **Sales Manager**（銷售經理）position at 3+3 Collection. I met Cherry while coordinating **an exhibition**（展覽）program in 2017. She was able to see my ability to **analyze**（分析）**trends**（趨勢）and results, to design and **implement**（實施）**strategic**（戰略性的）sales plans that expands company's **customer base**（客戶群）, and to build **long-lasting**（長期的）customer relationships, which is why she has **referred**（推薦）me to this role on your team."

③ 提出目標公司具新聞價值的時事

你申請的公司最近有沒有在新聞出現？假如有的話，那是否正面而且具新聞價值的時事？如是，你可以考慮在求職信的開首略略帶過這件事，以表示自己一直有留意對方，從而展示出自己的誠意。

小貼士

1 為避免產生不必要的誤解，請客觀描述具體的事件、重要的數據（notable statistics）或公司最近獲得的獎項（award）。

2 記得「點到即止」，切忌表現得過分「擦鞋」。

Useful words & expressions

be featured in xxx Magazine (v phr.)	出現在《xxx》雜誌上
be keenly interested in (v phr.)	對……有濃厚的興趣
commitment (n.)	承諾
four-digit revenue growth (n phr.)	四位數的收入增長
be inspired (v phr.)	被激發；受到啟發
track record (n phr.)	成績；記錄
to reduce costs by ___% (v phr.)	降低成本 ___%
to take on the _____ role (v phr.)	擔任 _____ 一職
to expand your company's growth (v phr.)	擴大公司的發展
motivation (n.)	動力
qualifications (n.)	資格

求職信開場白範例

"When I saw that KZC Ltd. was featured in Sunny Magazine last week for its **commitment**（承諾）to supply the highest quality, 100% organic, **Fair Trade**（公平貿易）, **freshly roasted**（新鮮烘焙的）coffee—all while experiencing **four-digit**（四位數的）**revenue growth**（收入增長）—I was **inspired**（受到啟發）. With my skills, experience, and **track record**（記錄）of reducing costs by 25% and promoting products and services to customers, I'm excited about the possibility of taking on the Marketing Assistant role to expand your company's growth. In this cover letter, I will elaborate on my **motivation**（動力）and **qualifications**（資格）required for this job opportunity."

④ 描述令人矚目的成就

人事經理瀏覽你的資歷時，目的是想要了解你是一名怎樣的員工。因此，你可以在求職信的開首突出個人成就和證明你的潛在價值，把你取得的成就寫在最前面，讓招聘者首先就能看到你的成績中最引人注目的方面。同時，記得描述與應徵的工作相關的經驗，讓面試官知道你有意善用自己的技能，在對方公司一展所長。

別把「個人成就（personal achievements）」寫成「職位描述（job descriptions）」。有的求職者純粹將工作職責重新描述一番，而絲毫未談及自己較突出的一面，結果給對方留下了「平平無奇」的感覺。

Useful words & expressions

to double (v.)	翻倍；加倍
Instagram followers (n phr.)	Instagram 的追隨者
Facebook ad campaigns (n phr.)	Facebook 廣告活動
to generate $_____ in revenue (v phr.)	產生 $ _____ 的收入
to bring my expertise to the _____ position at your company (v phr.)	將我的專業知識帶到貴公司 _____ 一職
marketing experience (n phr.)	營銷經驗
extensive (adj.)	廣泛的
diverse (adj.)	各種各樣的
to open up new markets (v phr.)	開闢新市場

to tap into my vast pool of contacts (v phr.)	進入我龐大的聯繫庫
to facilitate solid growth (v phr.)	促進穩健增長
emphasis (n.)	重視
to emphasize/emphasise (v.)	強調
employee development (n phr.)	員工發展
client satisfaction rate (n. phr.)	客戶滿意度
owes a lot to (v phr.)	歸功於

範例

求職信開場白範例（一）

"I was pleased finding the vacancy on ＿＿[www. 求職網站 .com]＿＿. As an Assistant Social Media Manager at my previous company, I have successfully increased sales from $95,000 to $155,000 within 4 months using Facebook ad campaigns. Besides, last month alone, I **doubled**（翻倍；加倍）that company's Instagram followers and ran three successful Instagram ad campaigns that generated $62K in **revenue**（收入）. I am keenly interested in the growth oriented position and would embrace the opportunity to **bring my expertise in expanding social reach to**（將我的專業知識帶去）the **Social Media Manager**（社交媒體經理）position at your company."

求職相關的問題

求職信開場白範例（二）

"LouisHK's **emphasis**（重視）on **employee development**（員工發展）is the reason why I am so excited about this position. My 99.9% **client satisfaction rate**（客戶滿意度）at the **previous company owes a lot to**（歸功於）my commitment to constant skills improvement. I'm thrilled to see where I could take your client within such a well-constructed system."

5 表達自己對工作的熱情

假如你在求職信中表現出一種冷漠的態度，你認為這樣能打動人心嗎？試想想，當每一位求職者的能力、背景都大同小異時，能使你突圍而出的關鍵是甚麼？熱情（Passion）就是決定性的關鍵。一般來説，公司都希望可以聘請得到具有強烈的職業道德且有潛質成為公司倡導者的員工。因此，如果你在求職信中能充分表現出自己對工作的熱情和活力的話，絕對可以在對方心中大大「加分」，從而增加脱穎而出的機會呢！

小貼士

1. 切忌阿諛奉承。老闆是不會想僱用一個只會「拍馬屁」的員工。因此，你應該表現得專業又成熟。
2. 切忌讓對方感到你「窮得只剩下熱誠」，這樣只會讓人感覺到你缺乏能力。記着，只有熱誠沒有能力是成不了大事的。

Useful words & expressions

be passionate about ___ (+NP/G)___ (v phr.)	對 _____ 充滿熱情
a long-term admirer (n phr.)	長期仰慕者
internship (n.)	實習
have a passion for ___ (+NP/G) ___ (v phr.)	對 _____ 充滿熱情
comprehensive (adj.)	全面的
imagination (n.)	想像力
creativity (n.)	創造力
expertise (n.)	專業知識
mission (n.)	使命
marketing services (n phr.)	營銷服務
inspiring (adj.)	鼓舞人心的
to contribute (v.)	貢獻
thrilled (adj.)	激動；興奮

求職信開場白範例

"As **a long-term admirer**（長期仰慕者）of your company, I am excited to submit my application for the **Product Management**（產品管理）internship at L&Y Tech posted on ___ [www. 求職網站 .com] ___. As a student at ABC University majoring in Digital Marketing, I have a passion for **multimedia design**（多媒體設計）. I believe I would be a good fit for the role owing to my **comprehensive**（全面的）imagination, creativity, and technical **expertise**（專長）. L&Y Tech's **mission**（使命）to be the first-choice digital marketing partner providing 360-degree **marketing services**（營銷服務）to businesses is **inspiring**（鼓舞人心的）, and I would be **thrilled**（激動；興奮）to be able **to contribute**（貢獻）to this mission."

6 説一個引人入勝的故事

建議可以適時為求職信增添些許（只是些許啊！）幽默感，讓求職信更生動、更具吸引力，從而讓審視者感動，並了解為甚麼你非這份工作不可。

小貼士

1 先就公司的背景進行一些研究,並留意該公司招聘廣告的語氣,再自行決定要不要嘗試走創意路線。

2 記得確保故事內容與你的來信主題息息相關。

Useful words & expressions

to take your business to the next level (v phr.)	使您的業務更上一層樓
to prove (v.)	證明
a safer approach (n phr.)	更安全的方法
critical (adj.)	關鍵的
under this time crunch (prep phr.)	在時間緊迫的情況下

範例

求職信開場白範例

"I **originally planned**(最初計劃)to submit my latest **credit card statement**(信用卡帳單)**to prove**(證明)my love for online shopping, but I thought **a safer approach**(更安全的方法)might be writing this cover letter, describing all the reasons why I'm the one who has the ability to take L & Y Collection's **business to the next level**(使⋯⋯的業務更上一層樓)."

你可以利用簡明扼要的表現出自己對該公司的價值觀和目標有深入了解，以誠意打動對方。切忌直接將公司網站的 mission statement（使命宣言）"copy and paste（搬字過紙）"否則會令自己形象大打折扣！

Useful words & expressions

to strive (to_____) (v.)	努力去 _____； 致力於 _____
entire community (n phr.)	整個社區
proactive planning (n phr.)	積極的計劃
key (n.)	關鍵
to set goals (v phr.)	設定目標
proactively (adv.)	主動地
to reach goals (v phr.)	達成 / 實現目標
to make a real contribution (v phr.)	真正貢獻
in an efficient manner (prep phr.)	高效地
commitment (n.)	承諾

求職信開場白範例

"I **not only**（不僅）**strive to**（致力於）impact clients but also my entire **community**（社區）. As a **financial advisor**（財務顧問）, I believe **proactive**（積極的）planning is the key to success. To me, my clients are the **captains**（船長）of their ship, and I am the **navigator**（領航員）of their ship. I enjoy taking the time to help set a course for their **goals**（目標）. Then, by **proactively**（主動地）partnering throughout their lives, I make sure those goals **are reached**（實現）. I would love to join your team of financial planners and make a real **contribution**（貢獻）to your business."

1.4 正文

一封好的求職信好比一頓令人垂涎欲滴的饕餮盛宴。如果說求職信的開場白（引言）是盛宴的頭盤部分，正文就是讓人望眼欲穿、期待不已的主菜了。在表明寫信的目的、交代應聘的職位及職位訊息來源後，就可着手介紹、甚至推銷自己，信函的正文應針對求職者自身的能力、優勢，以及所申請的職位要求作出具體的描述。

説到撰寫求職信的正文部分，不少人都會只忙於「曬冷」（顯示實力），把自己一切自認為值得驕傲的、與眾不同的，統統逐一羅列出來，深怕別人不知道你有多麼的優秀，就會把你看扁似的一樣。告訴別人你俱備那些才能，當然有助對方進一步了解你的背景，也更有助對方認同你是一個不可多得的人才。

在求職信正文中「曬冷」，不經篩選、盲目的把自己的才能和特質從頭訴說一遍，其實是一個大眾的通病。這不但未能把自己的特質凸顯出來，甚至有可能使求職信顯得贅長、欠重點，令對方沒耐性把求職信看畢。與其比誰更優秀，倒不如比誰更適合。

當然，你也可以把自己的優勢詳細的列出來，但謹記宜帶「針對性」！你可以概述與工作要求相關的技能、經驗和能力。例如，為甚麼你認為你是這個職位的最佳候選人？你所具備的技能與公司的需求有何直接或間接的關係等等。

■ 假如你是一名 fresh graduate（剛剛畢業的學生）

正文部分可以強調自己的學習成績，在校擔任過的職位（e.g. 學會、社團主席）和實習經驗（e.g. internships, part-time jobs）。

■ 假如你已經有工作經驗

正文部分可以略略介紹自己的學業背景，然後描述過往的工作經驗，盡量按照申請的職位提供一些相關的經驗。

表達「我擁有 _____ 的經驗」

實用句式 1

As you will note, I hold a _____ degree and have experience in _____ over _____ years.

您會注意到，我持有 _____ 學位，並且擁有 _____ 年 _____ 的經驗。

例句

As you will note, I hold a BEd in Early Childhood Education degree and have experience in childcare both on a personal level and professionally over 6 years.

您會注意到，我持有幼兒教育學士學位，並且擁有 6 年以上的個人和專業育兒經驗。

實用句式 2

My career has included _____ years working as a _____ with _____ companies.

我有 _____ 年在 _____ 公司擔任 _____ 的經驗。

例句

My career has included five years working as a software developer with software and technology companies.

我有 5 年在軟件和科技公司擔任項目軟件開發人員的經驗。

實用句式 3

As you will note, I have (rich) experience in _____.

您會注意到，我在 _____ 方面有（豐富的）經驗。

例句

As you will note, I have rich experience in tutoring Mathematics and Biology for Secondary level students.

您會注意到，我在中學數學和生物學輔導方面有豐富的經驗。

實用句式 4

From my resume, please note my ___-year experience in the _____ industry.

從我的履歷中，您會注意到我在 _____ 行業有 ___ 年的經驗。

例句

From my resume, please note my 6-year experience in the financial industry at multinational companies.

從我的履歷中，您會注意到我在跨國公司從事金融業有 6 年經驗。

列舉出主要的資格 / 成就 / 技能

The following achievements highlight the reason why I have confidence that I am the right candidate for this job:

以下的成就是我對自己有信心勝任這職位的原因：

以下是一些與技能和成就有關的具體例子：

Managed a team of 15 accounts assistants and interns to ensure all deadlines were met on time;

管理一個由 15 名客戶助理和實習生組成的團隊，以確保按時完成所有工作；

Met with the senior managers of each department in order to discuss their individual budgets and was able to reduce overall business expenditure by 20%, saving the company HKD650,000 a year;

與各部門的高級經理會面，以討論各自的預算，並能夠將整體業務支出減少 20%，從而每年為公司節省 650,000 港元；

Was nominated for the "Monthly Best Salesperson Award" and "Distinguished Salesperson Award" by my colleagues on multiple occasions;

多次被同事提名為「每月最佳推銷員」和「傑出推銷員」；

Modified the curriculum, which finally brought about increased student response and learning;

修改了課程內容，讓學生在課堂中有更踴躍的反應和學習動力；

Analyzed client portfolios by using Microsoft Access and was able to identify all the lower-performing accounts. With this data, I helped increase average client revenue by 16%;

通過使用 Microsoft Access 分析客戶的投資組合，並識別出所有效果欠佳的帳戶。藉助這些數據，我幫助將客戶的平均收入提高了 16%；

Served 80+ customers in one shift during an in-house campaign and cultivated 80% of them into actual buyers;

在公司廣告活動中，同一時段內服務了 80 多個客戶，並將 80%的客戶轉化成實際買家；

Won "Largest Percentage Growth Award" in 2020;

於 2020 年獲得「最大百分比增長獎」；

Introduced online and social media selling techniques, increasing the company's profits by 32%;

引入了在線和社交媒體銷售技巧，使公司的利潤提高了 32%；

Increased client base by 40% by being actively involved in marketing and sales promotions;

通過積極參與市場營銷和促銷活動，將客戶群增加了 40%；

Built long-lasting relationships with customers and ensured that their queries were dealt with within 24 hours;

與客戶建立長期的關係，並確保在 24 小時內處理他們的查詢；

Successfully handled 45 customers in one hour;

一小時內成功服務了 45 位客戶；

求職相關的問題

Improved customer services by looking out for loopholes from time to time and reporting them to the supervisor;

定期查找公司客戶服務系統的漏洞，並將其報告給主管以作出改善；

Trained 15 new retail sales assistants and interns, as part of their induction processes;

培訓出 15 名新的零售助理和實習生，以作為他們入職培訓的一部分；

Developed new spreadsheets in order to help produce the monthly management accounts efficiently, thereby reducing the production time from six days to four;

開發了新的電子表格，以助有效地處理每月的管理帳目，從而將處理時間從 6 天減少到 4 天；

Implemented a child care program that made provisions for students with special educational needs (SEN);

實施了一項兒童照顧計劃，該計劃為有特殊學習需要的兒童提供了保障；

實用句式 1

I believe I have the _____ experience you are looking for. I am confident that I would make a valuable addition to (Name of the Company).

我相信我有您所期盼的 _____ 經驗、雄心壯志和抱負，而且我知道我會成為（公司名稱）的寶貴員工。

例句

I believe I have the customer service experience, ambition, and drive you are looking for. I am confident that I would make a valuable addition to L&Y Collection Ltd.

我相信我有您所期盼的客戶服務經驗、雄心壯志和抱負，而且我知道我會成為 L & Y Collection Ltd 的寶貴員工。

With this understanding and my background, I am convinced that I would be an ideal candidate for the _____ position.

通過以上介紹，加上我的背景，我深信我會是 _____ 一職的理想人選。

例句

With this understanding and my background, I am convinced that I would be an ideal candidate for the Junior Shipping Clerk position.

通過以上介紹，加上我的背景，我深信我會是初級運輸文員一職的理想人選。

實用句式 3

I believe I have the qualifications you are searching for.

我相信我具備您所找尋的資歷。

實用句式 4

I am certain that I would make a valuable addition to (Name of the Company).

我深信我能成為（公司名稱）的寶貴員工。

1.5 結束語

在正文部分極力推銷自己一番後，終於到了求職信的尾聲，也就是結束語的部分。

撰寫求職信必須審慎嚴謹，因為求職信是求職者和招聘者第一次接觸的橋樑，一封由求職者親筆的求職信就代表了求職者自身的形象，求職信的內容、組織、風格某程度上也反映出求職者做人處事的作風。倘若把求職信撰寫到結束語的部分，就恍如「落雨收柴」般收結，到最尾就草草了事、倉促收筆的話，這種行為不但不討好，一不小心還很容易讓對方誤會你的為人，處理不善的話，更有可能在對方心目中留下做事「虎頭蛇尾」、「馬馬虎虎」等的不良印象。

撰寫求職信應該要和做人一樣，要貫徹始終，絕不能輕易鬆懈、有始無終。那麼，這部分具體該包含些甚麼內容呢？在結束語的部分，求職者除了總結一下上文重點，增加記憶點以外，也應該把握這次與 HR 或僱主首次接觸的機會，再次重申一次自己對爭取該職位空缺的熱誠，並且表現出自己對入職的強烈意願和渴求。

此外，筆者亦建議各求職者在結束語部分再次跟對方表明自己的決心，肯定地告訴他們自己極有信心能勝任該職位，承諾在入職後會好好珍惜機會、努力工作以回饋公司的知遇之恩，並懇請對方給予面試機會。

實用句式 1

Through all of these experiences, I believe that I would be able to _____ at your company. I welcome the opportunity to speak with you about _____. I look forward to hearing from you. Thank you for your consideration.

通過以上這些經驗，我相信我將能夠 _____。盼望能有機會與您會面並詳談 _____。感謝您考慮我，我期待得到您的回音。

例句

Through all of these experiences, I believe that I would be able to navigate the challenges successfully at your company. I welcome the opportunity to speak with you about my qualifications. I look forward to hearing from you. Thank you for your consideration.

通過以上這些經驗，我相信我將能夠成功應對　貴公司的挑戰。盼望能有機會與您會面並詳談我的資歷。感謝您考慮我，我期待得到您的回音。

I'm enthusiastic about seeing what I can do for (Name of the Company). Could we set aside some time to talk about _____?

我衷心希望能看到自己替（公司名稱）效力。請問可否騰出一些時間，讓我們討論一下 _____？

例句

I'm enthusiastic about seeing what I can do for YC Inc. Could we set aside some time to talk about ideas to raise your client transactions by 20% in a short period of time?

我衷心希望能看到自己替 YC Inc. 效力。請問可否騰出一些時間，讓我們討論如何可以在短時間內將您的客戶交易量提高 20%？

I would be glad to discuss how my skills in _____ can help (Name of the Company)'s customers succeed.

倘若能與您討論我在 _____ 方面的技能如何幫助（公司名稱）的客戶取得成功，我將感到非常高興。

例句

I would be glad to discuss how my skills in Facebook marketing and crisis management can help Alfento's customers succeed.

倘若能與您討論我在市場營銷及危機管理方面的技能如何幫助 Alfento's 的客戶取得成功，我將感到非常高興。

Could we schedule a call to discuss _____?

請問能否抽空讓我們在電話討論 _____？

例句

Could we schedule a call to discuss how I could help your current project outgrow expectations by 10-20% without additional costs?

請問能否抽空讓我們在電話討論如何能在不增加成本的情況下，使貴公司當前的項目超乎預期的 10-20％？

實用句式 5

My schedule is flexible and I look forward to arranging a time for an interview.

我的時間比較有彈性，並期待能安排面試的時間。

實用句式 6

Thank you for your attention. I look forward to hearing from you.

謝謝您的留意，並期待能進一步收到您的消息。

實用句式 7

Should you find my qualifications suitable to your needs, I will be happy to meet you at your convenience.

若您覺得我的條件符合您的要求，我很願意在您方便的時間與您會面。謝謝您的留意，並期待能進一步接到您的消息。

Part 1

求職相關的問題

實用句式 8

Thank you for your time and consideration. I look forward to speaking with you about this employment opportunity.

感謝您的時間和考慮。我期待着着與您談談這個職位。

實用句式 9

I would welcome the opportunity to discuss further the possibility of working for you in this position. I am available to do an interview when it is convenient for yourselves.

盼望能有機會與您進一步討論這職位。只要您方便，我隨時可以出席面試。

寫上自己的聯繫方式，以便對方聯繫你

實用句式 1

I can be reached anytime via email at (email address) or my cell phone, (phone number).

您可以隨時通過我的電郵（電郵地址）或我的聯絡電話（電話號碼）與我聯繫。

例句

I can be reached anytime via email at zephyryeung@ email. com or my cell phone, 9123-4567.

您可以隨時通過我的電郵 (zephyr.yeung@email.com) 或聯絡電話 (9123-4567) 與我聯繫。

實用句式 2

If you have any questions, I can be reached on either my mobile (phone number) or by email (email address).

如果您有任何疑問，可以通過我的聯絡電話（電話號碼）或電郵（電郵地址）與我聯繫。

例句

If you have any questions, I can be reached on either my mobile (9123-4567) or by email (zephyr.yeung@email.com).

如果您有任何疑問，可以通過我的聯絡電話（9123-4567）或電郵（zephyr.yeung@email.com）與我聯繫。

求職相關的問題

一般求職信都會附加個人履歷*，來幫助招聘者更好地了解應聘者的資歷。因此，在電郵結尾註明會附上簡歷。

* 下一章節 P.58 將會分享有關撰寫履歷表的技巧

告知對方參閱隨函附上履歷表

實用句式 1

Please see my resume for additional information on my experience.

請參閱我的履歷，以獲取更多與我的經歷有關的資料。

實用句式 2

Please find attached a copy of my C.V. which expands on my experience and achievements.

隨函附上我的履歷表副本，內裏描述了我的經驗和成就。

實用句式 3

Please find attached a copy of my resume and academic record.

隨函附上我的履歷表以及學歷成績表的副本。

實用句式 4

Enclosed you will find a letter of recommendation from my former employer.

隨函附上我前任僱主的推薦函。

實用句式 5

Attached please find an outline of my education and business training and a copy of letter of recommendation.

有關本人的學歷，工作經驗等項的概要，謹同函呈上一封推薦函，敬請察核。

1.6 下款 / 結尾敬語

求職信屬於較正式（formal）的文體。以下是結尾敬語（Closing Salutation）的例子：

較常見於英式英文

🖈 Yours faithfully,（當上款是 Dear Sir / Madam, 時）
🖈 Yours sincerely,（當上款使用姓氏時，e.g., Dear Ms Chan,）

📌 Sincerely Yours,

📌 Sincerely,

📌 Yours Truly,

以下這些 Closing Salutations 過於非正式（informal），
不適合用於求職信，敬請留意：

📌 Thanks,

📌 Take care,

📌 Yours,

📌 Best regards,（or "BR,"）

📌 Cheers,

📌 Best wishes,

撰寫求職信注意事項

📌 求職者應針對應聘公司的特點和職位要求，針對性地寫
cover letter。因此，落筆之前，應該再三閱讀招聘廣告
裏面的「職位描述（Job descriptions）」。

📌 在求職信的字裏行間，記得要透露你想為對方公司服務
的意願，多描述自己能為公司做甚麼，而非自己希望通
過該職位獲得甚麼利益和好處。簡單來説，就是以對方
角度出發。

求職英語一本通

📌 值得一提的是，在發送求職信函前，記得 proofread（校對）多幾次內容，切忌錯字連篇。否則，不但會給人輕率和缺乏誠意的印象，還會使對方對你的能力產生懷疑。

📌 適度的謙虛是美德，但過分的謙虛可能會帶來反效果 —— 讓對方認為你缺乏自信。因此，落筆前，記得先評估自己的能力和專長，好讓自己能實事求是地予以陳述。

📌 的確，適當地樹立信心能獲得別人的認同和讚賞。但同時，你也要注意，cover letter 中切忌「過分吹噓」。例如，不要說：「我能適應任何一種工作」。

範例

錯誤示範（一）

I heard that your company's business is not very good recently and I am fully capable of changing this situation.

聽説　貴公司最近以生意不太好，我完全有能力改變這種狀況。

求職相關的問題

錯誤示範（二）

I have investigated your company's situation, and I
have the ability to solve all the technical problems
you encounter.

我已經調查過　貴公司的情況了，你們遇到所有技
術問題我都能夠解決的。

📌 簡單來說，求職信中不易出現一些過分浮誇／吹嘘的字
眼。錯誤示範如下：

錯誤示範

- "I **guarantee**（保證）that ......"
- "Believe me. I can handle **all**（所有）these matters."
- "You can **completely**（徹底地）rely on me."

求職信應該要寫多長？

如果 cover letter 太短的話，可能無法清晰表達出求職者的
想法，也會讓對方感覺你誠意不足。然而，cover letter 太長的
話，又會有冗繁之嫌，可能引起對方的反感。（收件者有可
能每天要閱讀大量的求職信啊！）因此，一般來說，cover
letter 以 A4 紙的大半頁至一頁篇幅為宜。倘若你真的有很
多不得不提的內容需要詳加篇幅闡述，也不宜超過兩頁。

求職信範例（一）

Job Application: Sabrina Wong
for Social Media Manager (Ref: 1234)

Dear Hiring Manager,

I am writing to express my strong interest in the **Social Media Manager**（社交媒體經理）position open at MangoHK. As an Social Media Assistant Manager at my previous company, I have successfully increased sales from $80,000 to $160,000 within half year using Facebook ad campaigns. Besides, last month alone, I **doubled**（翻倍；加倍）that company's Instagram followers and ran three successful Instagram ad campaigns that generated $80K in **revenue**（收入）. I am keenly interested in this position and would embrace the opportunity to **bring my expertise in** expanding social reach **to**（將我……的專業知識帶去）the Social Media Manager position at your company.

應徵社交媒體經理（參考編號：1234）

致招聘經理：

本人對 MangoHK 社交媒體經理一職深感興趣，故特來函應徵。作為前公司的社交媒體助理經理，我透過一系列 Facebook 廣告在半年內成功地將銷售額從 8 萬元

提高到了 16 萬元。此外，僅於上個月，我已將該公司的 Instagram 追縱者增加了一倍，並成功開展了三個 Instagram 廣告系列，這些廣告系列帶來了 8 萬的收入。我對這個職位非常感興趣，希望能藉此機會將我在擴大社交範圍方面的專業知識帶到　貴公司的社交媒體經理職位。

As stated in your **job description**（職位描述）, you are looking for a Social Media Manager who is good at **collaborating**（合作）with people, particularly your upper management and sales staff. As you will note, I have rich experience in organizing **quarterly meetings**（季度會議）in which I presented marketing reports and sought analysis and feedback from the entire team. As an Assistant Social Media Manager at my previous company, I collaborated with the Director of Marketing and Producer of every company for which I worked. I believe that my experience in marketing and managing experience, as well as my ability to collaborate and communicate, make me a valuable addition to MangoHK.

如您的職位描述中所述，您正在尋找一位擅長合作、特別是與高層管理人員和銷售人員合作的社交媒體經理。您會注意到，我在組織季度會議方面擁有豐富的經驗，

在這些季度會議中，我負責介紹營銷報告，並尋求整個團隊的分析和反饋。作為我前公司的社交媒體助理經理，我負責與不同公司的營銷總監和製作人合作。我相信我在市場營銷和管理方面的經驗，加上協作和溝通能力，能使我成為 MangoHK 的寶貴員工。

Attached please find an outline of my education and business training and a copy of **letter of recommendation**（推薦函）. I would welcome the opportunity to discuss further the possibility of working for you in this position. I am available to do an interview when it is convenient for yourselves. I can be reached anytime via email at sabrinawong@email.com or my cell phone 9123-4567.

有關本人的學歷和工作經驗等項的概要，謹同函呈上一封推薦函，敬請察核。盼望能有機會與您進一步討論這職位。只要您方便，我隨時可以出席面試。您也可以隨時通過的電郵（sabrinawong@email.com）或我的聯絡電話（9123-4567）與我聯繫。

Yours faithfully,
Sabrina Wong
申請人
黃小美謹啟

求職相關的問題

求職成敗的關鍵之一，在於求職者的態度和決心，和在於是否能夠堅持做好求職的每一步。若果連撰寫履歷表這求職的初始步也未能做好，恐怕實在難以在這場競賽之中脫穎而出。一個職位空缺，隨時有可能同時吸引到數十甚至數百個求職者的目光，各求職者在看準目標後就會紛紛向有關公司遞交履歷表，希望能憑藉一份具個人特色的履歷表，打敗一眾對手，取得一個面試的機會，為心儀的職位空缺一戰。

在求職網頁上找到合適或者感興趣的職位空缺後，我們除了需要針對申請的職位來撰寫一封有力的求職信外，準備一份完整而具吸引力的履歷表也相當重要。僱主或 HR 通常在審視求職者的履歷表後，衡量該名求職者是否符合職位的要求，繼而考慮會否提供面試的機會。

由此可見，履歷表的重要性實在不容忽視，求職者必須用心編寫。求職者在求職的過程中，不妨經常幻想自己是一件商品，如果想吸引「買家」的注意，就必須懂得如何為自己做廣告。而 C.V.（Curriculum Vitae；履歷表）就像產品的廣告一樣，能夠讓僱主或 HR 對你有初步的認識，

甚至能讓他們有意欲進一步去了解你。懂得透過履歷表作自我推銷、凸顯個人優勢，才有可能取得一張面試的「入場券」。

C.V. 在執筆草擬 C.V. 前，求職者必須先「確認求職目標」，想清楚自己渴望和適合應徵甚麼工作再下筆編寫，草擬一份 C.V. 後，再具針對性地根據所應徵的職位調整 C.V. 內容。

記住：你的目標必須明確！在編撰 C.V. 時要時刻謹記自己的求職目標，這樣寫出來的 C.V. 才有可能貼合你所應徵的職位，內容才會與入職有關職位所需的資歷、特質等各方面的要求環環相扣。做好這一步，你的 C.V. 才會更有魅力，更能讓你獲得脫穎而出的機會。

小貼士

1 記得凸顯個人與所應徵職務間的關係
C.V. 如果沒有凸顯個人與所應徵職務間的關係，就很容易被淹沒在眾多的履歷當中，結果連親自向招聘者推銷自己的機會都沒有了。

2 時時刻刻詢問自己：「我的所學所能是否符合應聘公司的需要？」
在撰寫 C.V. 的過程中，切忌忘形地詳細介紹自己的背景，導致履歷內容不符合公司需求，你的 C.V. 亦隨之石沉大海。

英文履歷表的六個部分

1 求職者的聯繫方式
Contact Information

2 求職者的求職目標
Job Objective

3 求職者的工作經驗
Work Experience

4 求職者的教育背景
Education Background

5 求職者的電腦、語言及其他技能
Computer Skills, Language Skills, Other Skills

6 推薦人的相關訊息（如適用）
References

這六個部分的順序可以根據求職者的自身情況進行排列，也可根據應聘職位的不同進行調整。

有一定工作經驗的求職者

對於有一定工作經驗的求職者來說，工作經驗（work experience）一欄應放在教育背景（education）之前。

剛剛畢業的 fresh graduates

對於初出茅廬的畢業生來說，教育背景（education）一欄應放在工作經驗（work experience）之前。

接下來，筆者會一一介紹如何撰寫這六個部分的內容。

2.1 求職者的聯繫方式

這部分內容應包括求職者的姓名（Name）、電郵地址（email address）、聯絡電話（contact number）等。假如你有 Linkedin 帳號，而且內含有用的資訊的話，也可以把其鏈接放在這裏。

範例

Chris Chan

Email: chrischan@email.com

Phone: (+852) 9123-4567

Linkedin: linkedin.com/in/yourprofile

2.2 求職者的求職目標

「目標陳述（Objective Statement）」是就事業願景的介紹性陳述，一般放在履歷表的開首，簡單説明申請這個職位的原因、工作願景，以及你希望將來在該公司達到的目標。目標陳述寫得好，讓對方發現你的能力與這個職位有多匹配才是重中之重，絕對能為你的 C.V. 畫龍點睛，加分再加分！

challenging (adj.)	具有挑戰性的
an executive level (n phr.)	行政級別；高級
my extensive _____(e.g. marketing) experience (n phr.)	我豐富的 _____ 經驗
to utilize (v.)	利用
to gain further experience (v phr.)	以獲得更多經驗
to enhance (v.)	加強
productivity (n.)	生產力
reputation (n.)	聲譽
to leverage (v.)	利用
opportunity (n.)	機會
to benefit (v.)	使……得益

撰寫目標陳述（Objective statement）必學句型

必學句型 1

My goal/objective is to...
我的目標是……

■ 必學句型 2

📌 I am seeking...
我正在尋找……

■ 必學句型 3

📌 I am looking at new opportunities to...
我正在尋找新的機會去……

■ 必學句型 4

📌 My career objective is to...
我的職業目標是……

■ 必學句型 5

📌 Equipped with _____-year experience in _____ ,
I am seeking a challenging position in _____.
我擁有 _____ 年的 _____ 經驗，並正在
_____ 行業尋求一個具有挑戰性的職位。

目標陳述 (Objective statement) 範例參考

語氣毫不專業的錯誤示範

Enthusiastic waitstaff applicant with not much experience yet but very willing to learn. I really want to work at your hotel so please hire me. You won't have to worry about my ability because I am so hard-working.

熱情的服務員申請人，雖然經驗不足，但是非常願意學習。我真的很想在您的酒店工作，所以請僱用我。您不必擔心我的能力，因為我很努力。

Hard-working waiter, seeking to use proven customer service skills to foster dining excellence at The Nonos'.
勤奮的服務生，渴望能利用客戶服務經驗來提升 Nonos' 餐廳的用餐質量。

以下是筆者為不同行業（如銷售、管理、媒體傳播、文員、行政管理、市場營銷、物業管理、人力資源、資訊科技、公共關係、Fresh graduates 等）準備的目標陳述（Objective statement）範例：

Sales（銷售）

My career objective is to obtain a position as a sales representative with a local company. My eventual goal is to move into a marketing management position with involvement in **training**（培訓）, advertising, and **marketing research**（市場研究）.
我的職業目標是獲得本地公司的銷售代表職位。我最終的目標是進入市場管理職位，並參與培訓、廣告和市場研究。

求職英語一本通

64

Management (管理)

My objective is to obtain a position in which I can use my **extensive** (廣泛;豐富的) management experience.

我的目標是獲得一個讓我可以運用豐富管理經驗的職位。

Media communications (媒體傳播)

Equipped with 5-year experience in media communications, I am seeking a challenging position in an Entertainment channel.

我擁有 5 年的媒體傳播經驗,並正在娛樂行業尋求一個具有挑戰性的職位。

Office Staff (辦公室職員;文員)

My objective is to obtain a position in a professional office environment where my skills are valued and can benefit the organization.

我的目標是在專業的辦公環境中工作,同時希望個人技能得到重視,從而有效地服務公司。

求職相關的問題

Executive management（行政管理；高級管理層）

My goal is to further my professional career with an **executive level**（行政級別；高級）management position in **a world class**（世界級的）company.
我的目標是在世界級公司擔任高級管理職位，進一步提升自己。

My career objective is to obtain a challenging leadership position because I continually strive for personal growth in every aspect of my career.
我的職業目標是獲得一個具有挑戰性的領導職位，因為我在各個方面都在不斷追求個人成長。

Marketing（市場營銷）

I am seeking a challenging position in a marketing firm where my extensive experience and creativity will be fully utilized.
我正從各行銷公司中尋找一個具挑戰性的職位，使我的豐富經驗和創意得以完全發揮。

My goal is to become associated with a company where I can **utilize**（利用）my skills and experience in **enhancing**（提高）its **productivity**（生產力）and **reputation**（聲譽）.

我的目標是在一家容許我利用我的技能和經驗且同時提高公司的生產力和聲譽的公司工作。

My objective is to obtain a position which will allow me to utilize my writing and organization skills.

我正尋求一個可容許我有效利用我的寫作及組織技巧的職位。

Property Management（物業管理）

I am looking at new opportunities **to leverage**（利用）my 5 years of professional property **management**（管理）experience to increase company profits through favorable sales.

我正在尋找新的機會來利用我 5 年的專業物業管理經驗，通過有利的銷售來增加公司利潤。

Human Resources（人力資源）

I am seeking a position as an assistant in the HR department that will utilize my knowledge of **labor relations**（勞資關係）, benefit programs, **wage administration**（工資管理）, and employment law. My eventual goal is to advance to the position of personnel manager.

求職相關的問題

我正在尋找人力資源部門的助理職位，以善用我對勞資關係、福利計劃、工資管理和僱傭法的知識。我的最終目標是晉升為人事經理。

I am looking at new opportunities **to utilize**（利用）my skill and experience in a Human Resource capacity.
我正在尋找新的機會來利用我在人力資源方面的技能和經驗。

Information Technology（資訊科技）

I am desiring a position as a programmer or systems analyst utilizing quantitative and mathematical training. I have special interest in marketing and financial applications.
我希望善用定量和數學培訓的經驗，並擔任程序員或系統分析員一職。我對市場營銷和金融應用特別感興趣。

Public Relations（公共關係）

My career objective is to obtain a position in public relations which will allow me to utilize my superior language skills, problem solving abilities and task management skills, and to contribute to the success of the organization.

我的職業目標是獲得一個公關方面的職位，以使我能夠利用自己熟練的語言技能、解難能力和任務管理技能，並貢獻組織。

Fresh graduates（剛畢業的社會新鮮人）

Coming with a degree in Human Resource Management, I am seeking an **entry-level**（入門級）human resources assistant position at a **dynamic**（充滿活力的）organization.

本人擁有人力資源管理學位，並正在充滿活力的公司中尋求一個入門級的人力資源助理職位。

A student-focused（以學生為中心的）educator with a Bachelor degree in Mathematics Education seeking an entry-level teacher position at a local high school.

我是一名以學生為中心的教育工作者，並擁有數學教育學士學位。我正在尋找尋找本地入門級教師的職位。

A fresh graduate of Engineering currently looking for an entry-level software developer position to ensure that system software functions efficiently.

應屆工程專業的畢業生目前正在尋找入門級軟件開發人員的職位，以確保公司系統軟件能有效地運行。

求職相關的問題

2.3 求職者的工作經驗

求職者在撰寫自己的 work experience 這部分內容時，應注意以下幾點：

第一點

> 採取「倒敘」的形式描述。先描述最近的工作經歷，再寫以往的工作經歷。

求職者近期做過的工作是 HR 最關注的部分，因為這最能體現求職者的能力和對業務的熟悉程度。（記住，HR 沒有那麼多時間在簡歷上找自己需要的訊息，所以求職者在寫簡歷時就要做到可以讓 HR 一眼看到重要的內容。不相關的工作經歷盡量少提或一筆帶過。）

例子

🔖 L&Y Collection LTD.
Sales Representatice（May 2017 - July 2020）

🔖 Boutique Radar
Sales Assistant（May 2015 - April 2017）

🔖 KZC Gourmet
Sales Assistant（Mar 2013 - April 2015）

問：當兩段工作經驗的時間重疊了怎麼辦？

答：以結束時間為準排序。

例子

📌 Gourmet Street
Sales Representative（May 2017 - March 2021）

📌 Powerful Cuisine
Part-time Sales Assistant（May 2015 - April 2017）

📌 Edmond Fiesta
Part-time Sales Assistant（Mar 2015 - November 2016）

第二點

描述自己的工作經驗時，不要單單列舉工作職責或負責的項目。除此之外，求職者亦應該「具體描述」所完成的任務或項目，包括一些過往的業績和成就。

錯誤示範

✗ Initiated a series of marketing campaigns
發起了一系列的營銷活動

良好示範

✓ Initiated a series of marketing campaigns **including print, digital, and social media analysis, and content for direct mail campaigns and blogs**
發起了一系列營銷活動，包括印刷、電子和社交媒體分析，以及透過在郵件和博客直接傳送推銷活動訊息。

求職相關的問題

Awarded "Outstanding Achievement" trophy for consistently performing above average sales.

因持續表現高於平均水平而獲得「傑出成就」獎。

Trained over 10 new employees in industry knowledge, sales presentation, and closing strategies.

培訓了 10 多位新員工，並為他們提供行業知識、銷售介紹技巧和促使成交策略。

第三點

介紹自己在某組織的工作經驗時，應按照「重要訊息優先」的原則，將最重要的成就以及較獨特的事蹟寫在前面。

第四點

在描述自己的工作成就時，盡量使用「具體的數字」，以突出成就。例如具體寫出客戶增加的具體數字、銷售額增長的具體百分比等。求職者應盡量避免使用 "a lot of", "a number of", "many", "some" 等模糊的字眼。

錯誤示範

✗ Analyzed the specific needs of customers via careful surveys to develop data driven pitches, increasing **a lot of** profits over two years.

通過仔細調查來分析客戶的特定需求，以開發以數據為依據的營銷策略，並在兩年內增加了很多利潤。

良好示範

✓ Analyzed the specific needs of customers via careful surveys to develop data driven pitches, increasing profits **by 15%** over two years.

通過仔細調查來分析客戶的特定需求，以開發以數據為依據的營銷策略，並在兩年內使利潤增長 15%。

例子 1

Discovered, negotiated, and secured new relationships with local and overseas organizations, resulting in a significant increase in profitability by 15 to 25% annually.

發掘、談判，並確保公司與本地和海外組織的關係，從而使利潤率每年顯著提高 15% 到 25%。

例子 2

Assisted clients with business plan, branding, advertising and marketing, increasing monthly sales from HKD$120,000 to HKD$250,000 in three months.

協助客戶制定商業計劃、建立品牌、做廣告和市場營銷，並在 3 個月內將月銷售額從 12 萬港元增加到 25 萬港元。

例子 3

Increased followers on social media by 165% on average, resulting in $120,000 in increased sales.

社交媒體上的追隨者平均增加 165%，銷售額亦隨即增加了 12 萬元。

第五點

描述自己的職責時，避免使用過分複雜的句式，用精簡的英文短句敘述即可。

第六點

在描述自己過往的工作經歷時，應該用甚麼時態 (tense)？普遍使用過去式 (Simple Past Tense) 描述過去經驗。

例子

Initiated a series of marketing campaigns including print, digital, and social media analysis, and content for direct mail campaigns and blogs

- Awarded "Outstanding Achievement" trophy for consistently performing above average sales
- Trained over 10 new employees in industry knowledge, sales presentation, and closing strategies
- Analyzed the specific needs of customers via careful surveys to develop data driven pitches, increasing profits by 15% over two years
- Discovered, negotiated, and secured new relationships with local and overseas organizations, resulting in a significant increase in profitability by 15 to 25% annually
- Assisted clients with business plan, branding, advertising and marketing, increasing monthly sales from HKD$120,000 to HKD$250,000 in three months
- Increased followers on social media by 165% on average, resulting in $120,000 in increased sales

第七點

撰寫 C.V. 運用的詞彙比平日書寫時運用的要更「強而有力」。

想要寫出專業的、令人眼前一亮的感覺，你可以從動詞的應用着手。求職者不妨替自己的 C.V. 換上以下的「精選動詞」，讓僱主眼前一亮：

讓僱主眼前一亮的 78 個「精選動詞」

Achieved 達成	Acquired 取得；獲得
Analyzed 分析	Assemble 集合；聚集；組裝
Assessed 評估；評價	Attained 實現；獲得；取得
Audited 審計；審核	Authored 撰寫
Authorized 授權	Awarded 榮獲
Briefed 介紹；簡介	Calculated 計算
Co-authored 合着	Completed 完成
Conveyed 傳達	Convinced 說服
Counseled 忠告；輔導	Critiqued 批評
Defined 批評	Delegated 委託
Designed 設計	Demonstrated 展示；證明
Devoted 貢獻	Developed 發展 / 展開
Dispatched 分派	Discovered 發現
Diversified 使……多元化	Documented 批評
Edited 編輯	Enforced 強制；執行
Enhanced 增強 / 提升	Ensured 確保
Evaluated 評價；評估	Examine 探討；檢查
Exceeded 突破	Executed 執行
Explored 探索；探究	Forecasted 預報；預測

Generated 產生	Identified 鑑定；辨認
Illustrated 說明；展示	Implemented 實施
Increased 增加 / 提升	Initiated 發起
Inspected 考察；檢查	Interpreted 解讀
Investigated 探討；調查	Itemized 分項
Lobbied 遊說	Measured 測量
Monitored 監測；監控	Negotiated 協商；磋商
Outperformed 跑贏大市	Partnered 成為合作夥伴關係
Persuaded 說服	Pioneered 開創
Promoted 促進推動	Promoted 推銷
Publicized 公示；公佈	Reached 達到
Researched 研究	Reviewed 審查
Scrutinized 仔細檢查；審查	Secured 確保；擔保
Showcased 展示	Spearheaded 率先帶領
Standardized 使……標準化	Succeeded 成功
Surpassed 超越；超過	Surveyed 調查
Targeted 目標為……	Tested 測試
Tracked 追蹤	Transformed 改造
Unified 統一	Upgraded 升級
Utilized 利用	Validated 驗證

2.4 求職者的教育背景

對於剛剛畢業的求職者來說，教育背景（Education Background）是履歷中非常重要的一部分。一個好的教育背景是拿到 offer 的關鍵之一。（註：好的教育背景 ≠ 好的學校，而是在於你如何描述你的教育背景）在履歷表中，教育背景一般也包括「必有訊息（necessary information）」和「可選訊息（optional information）」。

■ 必有訊息（necessary information）

📌 就讀日期（Date）

📌 畢業年份（如適用）（Graduation year）

📌 院校名稱（Name of the institution）

📌 專業 / 類別（Your field of study）
（例如：engineering 工程、marketing 市場營銷、event management 活動管理等）

📌 學位程度（Degree level）
（例如：associate degree 副學士、bachelor degree 學士、postgraduate degree 研究生等）

📌 學位名稱（Degree title）
（例如：BBA (Hons) in Marketing, BEd (Hons) in Mathematics）

可選訊息（optional information）

📌 成績／排名（Results／ranking）
📌 獲獎情況（Awards）
📌 研究方向（Research direction）
📌 研究項目（Research project）
📌 其他活動（Other activities）

✗ 例子

BBA (Hons) in Marketing

University of Kowloon 2017 - 2021

📌 Completed all coursework so far

📌 * GPA 3.0

*是否需要描述自己的成績如 GPA？如果你的成績特別優異（例如：3.5/4.0 以上），或者應聘公司要求，不妨把這項資料寫進去。假如你的成績平平無奇，還是不要在 C.V. 提及成績，這不但對求職毫無幫助，甚至會成為扣分點。

✓ 例子

BBA (Hons) in Marketing

University of Kowloon

📌 2016 - 2021 (Graduating in May)

📌 Awarded the most entrepreneurial student in Strategic Marketing in 2020

2.5 求職者的電腦、語言及其他技能

求職者除了要列舉自己的 Work Experience 和 Education Background 外，如工作需要，你還可以在履歷表中介紹自己的其他才能，例如「電腦水平」、「語文水平」，以及其他與應聘職位相關的技能。

具體而言，這些技能一般可分為硬技能（hard skills）和軟技能（soft skills）兩種。Hard skills 包括「電腦」、「銷售」等各種專業技能；soft skills 包括「語文水平」、「溝通能力」、「人際關係」等。

硬技能（hard skills）

假如求職者想描述自己熟練掌握某種 software（軟件），可以用 "frequent user of + 軟件名稱" 來表達。然而，假如你對該軟件的認知只是一知半解的話，千萬不要寫在 C.V.！因為面試時，對方很可能會隨機地問你一些有關該軟件的操作方法，如果到時候問到你「口啞啞」，那就實在是太尷尬了。

> **範例**

📌 Frequent user of Microsoft Office programs such as Word, Excel, Publisher and PowerPoint

📌 Frequent user of EViews, Minitab, SPSS

電腦技巧（Computer Skills）

在當今的就業市場上，基本上任何行業都必須具備一定的電腦技巧。

■ 「電腦技巧」相關的常見軟件 / 技能

- MS Office: Word, Outlook, Powerpoint, OneNote, Access
- Google Drive
- Spreadsheets
- Presentations / Slideshows
- Database Management
- Quickbooks
- Social media
- Typing

■ 「編程技巧（programming skills）」相關的常見軟件 / 技能

- Python
- Java
- iOS/Swift
- PHP
- MySQL
- SQL
- C#
- JavaScript
- C++

設計技巧（Design Skills）

「圖形設計技巧」相關的常見軟件 / 技能

- Acrobat
- Photoshop
- Illustrator
- InDesign
- UX/UI design
- UX research
- Data visualization
- Color theory
- HTML / CSS
- Sketching
- Typography
- Print design
- Layout

營銷技巧（Marketing Skills）

營銷硬技能對於媒體（media）、廣告（advertising）、社交媒體（social media）、電子商務（e-commerce）和產品管理（product management）方面具有重大的價值。

■ 「營銷技巧」相關的常見軟件 / 技能

📌 Google Analytics and Google Search Console

📌 AdWords, Facebook Paid Ads

📌 SEO / SEM: Ahrefs, SEMRush, SEO Power Suite

📌 PPC

📌 Social media marketing and paid social media advertising

📌 CRO and A/B testing

📌 Email marketing and automation

📌 HubSpot, Aritic PinPoint, ONTRAPORT, Infusionsoft

📌 Funnel management

📌 UX Design

📌 Data visualization

分析能力（Analytical Skills）

分析技能指的是「收集數據（gathering data）」、「分析數據（analyzing data）」、「解讀含義（deciphering the meaning）」的技能。

■ 「分析能力」相關的常見軟件 / 技能

📌 Research

📌 Forecasting

📌 Data mining

📌 Resource management

📌 Diagnostics

- Creativity
- Theorizing
- Data engineering
- Database management
- Reporting

軟技能（soft skills）

此外，語言能力是最容易在面試中被測試的，所以求職者要如實描述自己的語言水平，切忌過分誇耀。

在描述 Language Abilities（語言能力）時，第一個項目寫你的母語，例如 Cantonese 或 Chinese（*記得寫 native 而非 fluent 或是 advanced）。接下來就是寫你的「第二語言（Second language）」，或者其次流利的語言，例如英文。最後就是寫你的第三語言（Third language）或其他略懂一二的語言。

描述語言能力常用字詞

- 母語："native"
- 接近母語："fluent" 或 "near native"

（"Near native" 是接近母語人士的能力，但是因為這不是他的母語，所以最高只能寫到 "near native"。"Fluent" 比 "near native" 低一點，意思是「流利但還不到 "near native"」）

📌 再下來一點可以寫 "excellent command of English" / "highly proficient in spoken and written English"

📌 再下來一點可以寫 "good command of English" / "good working knowledge of English" / "intermediate"

📌 如果自問自己的英語能力只是「有限公司（i.e. 略懂英語）」，就可以寫 "basic"

📌 如果能夠應付日常溝通，可寫 "conversational" / "working knowledge of English"

📌 如果只是剛開始學，可以寫 "beginner"

範例

Language Abilities:

Bilingual in Cantonese and English, knowledge of Spanish, lived in Barcelona for one year.
具廣東話和英文雙語能力，略懂西班牙語，曾在巴塞隆拿居住一年。

Mandarin (native speaker), English (fluent), Japanese (studied)
普通話（母語），英語（流利），日語（學過）

這通常是學術履歷（C.V.）的最後一部分。列出 3-5 位專業領域或學術界的推薦人，這些推薦人可以證明你的能力和資歷，必要時也可提供你具備這些特質的相關證明。

列出推薦人的姓名、專業頭銜、聯繫方式（電話和 email 即可）。不需要按照英文字母順序排列推薦人，而是依照他們與你申請職位的相關程度和影響力來排列。

範例

	Dr. Wendy Lai
Title（職位）：	Head of Operations
Company/ Organization name（公司 / 組織名稱）：	Parole Banking
Address（地址）：	Room 101A, Block A, Happy Buildings, 1, Apple Road, Mong Kok, Kowloon
Contact number（聯絡電話）：	(+852) 2123-4567
Email address（電郵地址）：	wendylai@parolebanking.com

小貼士

1 不要把年代久遠的訊息也寫進 C.V.

如果你已經大學畢業了，甚至已經踏出社會一段日子，一般來說，初中、高中的資訊就沒必要寫進 C.V 了。

2 不必把成績也寫進 C.V.

除非你的成績真的出色過人，或者應聘公司要求，否則，真的沒必要把 GPA 也寫進 C.V.。假如你的成績平平無奇，這對求職毫無幫助，甚至會成為扣分點。

3 履歷表保持在一頁之內

出色的履歷表，最好是保持在一頁之內。如果你申請的職位比較高級，那麼可以把標準放寬到兩頁。履歷表的目的就是概括最令人印象深刻和有價值的成就、能力。在這一至二頁中應充分說明「Who are you?（你是誰）」、「What do you want to do?（你需要甚麼）」以及「What have you done?（你曾做過甚麼）」。

4 校對、校對、再校對！

C.V. 中應避免任何錯字、拼字錯誤和文法、標點符號、大小寫錯誤。只要一或兩個錯誤，就足以讓你的 C.V. 石沉大海。

5 省略主語（subject）

履歷表內的句子不須強加主語（subject），尤其忌諱出現 "I" 這個第一人稱，因為這會使人感覺幼稚膚淺。

Chelsea Choi

Contact Details	
Contact no. :	(852) 9123-4567
Email :	Chelsea_choi@email.com

Equipped with 5-year experience in social media management, I am seeking a challenging position in which I can use my extensive management experience.

Summary

- Rich experience in managing professional social media accounts
- Ability to work closely with clients to develop and execute a proactive, social content calendar, managing all phases digital marketing initiatives from concept through delivery and optimization
- Excellent customer service skills and attention to detail

Key accomplishments

- Increased inbound traffic for clients' websites by up to 52%
- Developed content for clients' websites
- Applied analytics tools to boost websites' reach
- Developed engaged community of followers for clients

Education

Graduate Year:	2016
Institute/University:	ABC University
Qualification:	Master of Business Administration (Specialization: Marketing)
Graduate Year:	2014
Institute/University:	XYZ University
Qualification:	Bachelor of Business Administration (Specialization: Marketing)

Work Experience

Period	Position	Name of School / Company	Job Description
June 2017- Mar 2021	Assistant Social Media Manager (Full-time)	A&B Firm	• Created occasional posts to cross promote events hosted by other departments • Reviewed analytics to assess success; • Prepared reports on campaigns based on analytics; • Recommended improvements for future ads; • Utilized analytics tools to gauge the success of campaigns; • Updated posts to include relevant keywords for search engine optimization
Sept 2015 - May 2017	Assistant Social Media Manager (Part-time)	C&C Corporation	• Applied optimization techniques to improve audience engagement; • Maintained momentum in inbound marketing campaigns; • Fostered enthusiasm for social media amongst sales and marketing teams

Language Abilities

Cantonese (Native), **English** (Fluent), **Mandarin** (Fluent)

Key Skills

Marketing Analytics, Social Media Management, Google Analytics, Google AdWords, Strategic Planning, Business Development

Reference

Dr. **Wendy Lai** from **Parole Banking**
Head of Operations
Room 101A, Block A, Happy Buildings, 1, Apple Road, Mong Kok, Kowloon
(+852) 2123-4567 | wendylai@parolebanking.com

Useful words & phrases

to develop 開發	to execute 執行
inbound Traffic 入站流量	to boost websites' reach 提高網站的覆蓋率
occasional 定期的；間中的	to assess 評估
to gauge 衡量	momentum 氣勢；勢頭
audience engagement 受眾參與度	search engine optimization (SEO) 搜索引擎優化
enthusiasm 熱情	

Part 1

求職相關的問題

03 如何回覆面試邀請

各公司或企業的僱主或 HR 在審視各求職者所遞交的申請後，便會憑藉求職者所遞交的資料（包括求職信、履歷表等相關的文件）進行篩選，按照職位空缺的要求選出合適的求職者，並向他們發送正式的面試邀請。正所謂「各處鄉村各處例」，每一間公司都有他們的文化，在處理招聘事宜上的做法也有一定的差異。然而，一般而言各公司或企業通知求職者前來面試的方式主要有兩種：(1) 電話通知、(2) 電郵通知。

相信各求職者在遞交求職申請後的每一天都過得相當不容易，每天都抱着忐忑的心不停刷新郵件通知，或是總情不自禁地時刻關注着電話的每一個動靜。捱過了一段漫長又痛苦的等待後，終於收到晝思夜想的面試通知。不論你是透過電話或是電郵方式收到通知，在收到面試邀請後都請務必注意自己的言談，要表現得大方得體、莊重得宜，這有助求職者在正式與僱主或 HR 見面前，建立一個美好的形象，為面試打好根基，進一步邁向求職成功的軌道。

在考慮求職者是不是一個合適的人選時，求職者自身的技能和資格固然是重要的考慮因素，然而他們的個人形象也是取決他們成敗的一大因素之。與招聘人員或招聘經理的溝通方式正好直接影響對方對求職者的直觀印象，所以請審慎對待任何一次口頭和書面的交流，時刻保持警惕，表現出誠懇的態度。

總而言之，在招聘的過程中，在每一次與對方公司打交道的時候，你都必須保持應有的風度，在言行舉止上遵守適當的禮節，這樣才可為自己的形象大大加分。

成功秘訣

1 在上款使用聯絡人的姓名，而非 "Dear Sir/ Madam,"。

2 在信件開首必須先答謝對方給予面試機會。

3 仔細檢查電郵有沒有錯別字或語法問題，並確保收件人資料正確無誤。

4 （如適用）詢問面試官是否希望你帶上任何文件（如：畢業證書、成績單、以前工作的作品樣本）。

以下是透過電郵回應面試邀請的實用句式和電郵範例：

求職相關的問題

3.1 透過電郵回覆面試邀請

I would like to thank you for granting me the opportunity for an interview. I will be meeting up with you at (Company Name) for the interview at (Time) on (Date).

感謝　貴公司給予機會面試，我將於（日期、時間）在（公司名稱）與您見面，謝謝您。

例句

I would like to thank you for granting me the opportunity for an interview. I will be meeting up with you at L&Y Collection for the interview at 10:30 am on 28th May, 2021.

感謝　貴公司給予機會面試，我將於 2021 年 5 月 28 日上午 10:30 在 L&Y Collection 與您見面，謝謝您。

Yes, I very much would like to interview with you at (Time) on (Date).

是的，我非常期待在（日期）（時間）與您會面。

例句

Yes, I very much would like to interview with you at 10:30 am on 28th May, 2021.

是的，我非常期待在 2021 年 5 月 28 日上午 10:30 與您會面。

Thank you for your consideration and the invitation to interview for the (Position) at (Company Name). I appreciate the opportunity and I look forward to meeting with you on (date) at (time) to discuss this position in more detail.

謝謝您考慮我的申請，並就（職位）一職邀請我前來（公司名稱）參加面試。我很高興能有這機會，並期待着與您在（日期）（時間）見面，以更詳細地討論這職位。

Thank you for your consideration and the invitation to interview for the Event Manager position at L&Y Collection. I appreciate the opportunity and I look forward to meeting with you on 28th May, 2021 at 2pm to discuss this position in more detail.

謝謝您考慮我的申請，並就活動經理一職邀請我前來 L & Y Collection 參加面試。我很高興能有這機會，並期待着與您在 2021 年 5 月 28 日下午 2 時見面，以更詳細地討論這職位。

實用句式 4

Thank you for getting back to me and presenting me with this opportunity for an interview. I have confidence that I am an ideal candidate for the (Position). I look forward to meeting with you on (date) at (time) to discuss this position in more detail.

感謝您回覆我的申請，並給予這次面試的機會。我有信心我會是（職位）的理想人選。我期待在（時間）（日期）與您會面，以更詳細地討論這個職位。

例句

Thank you for getting back to me and presenting me with this opportunity for an interview. I have confidence that I am an ideal candidate for the Teaching Assistant position at C & C Tutorial Center. I look forward to meeting with you on 6th November at 3 p.m. to discuss this position in more detail.

感謝您回覆我的申請，並給予這次面試的機會。我有信心我會是教學助理一職的理想人選。我期待在 11 月 6 日下午 3 時與您會面，以更詳細地討論這個職位。

實用句式 5

Please let me know if there is any additional information you would like for me to provide or if there are any documents or certificates you would like me to bring on the day of the interview. Thanks!

如果你需要我於面試當天攜帶任何文件或證明，煩請告知我。謝謝！

實用句式 6

At your convenience, please let me know when you have openings in your schedule.

在您方便的時候，煩請告知我您甚麼時候比較方面安排面試。

實用句式 7

Although I currently work standard business hours, I am available for interviews _____ (time that is convenient for you). Is it possible to schedule an interview during these times?

儘管我目前的工作時間是標準的上班時間，但我可以在（你方便面試的時間）進行面試。請問您是否方便在這些時段安排面試？

例句

Although I currently work standard business hours, I am available for interviews before 10 a.m. and after 5 p.m. Is it possible to schedule an interview during these times?

儘管我目前的工作時間是標準的上班時間，但我可以在上午 10 時之前和下午 5 時之後進行面試。請問您是否方便在這些時段安排面試？

回應面試邀請電郵範例（一）

Dear Mr. Chan,

Thank you for getting back to me and presenting me with this opportunity for an interview. I have confidence that I am an ideal candidate for the **Property Consultant Trainee**（房地產顧問見習生）position at ABC Property Agent. I look forward to meeting with you on 5th June at 3 p.m. to discuss this position in more detail.

Please let me know if there is any additional information you would like for me to provide or if there are any documents or certificates you would like me to bring on the day of the interview.

Yours sincerely,

Kenny Chan

Phone: (+852) 9123-4567

求職相關的問題

回應面試邀請電郵範例（二）

Dear Mr. Yeung,

I received an email from your secretary Emily this morning requesting that I contact you to schedule an interview for the **Guest Services Agent**（客戶服務代理）role at Hotel Comfy. Thank you so much for granting me the opportunity for an interview.

At your convenience, please let me know when you have openings in your schedule. Although I currently work standard business hours, I am available for interviews before 10 a.m. and after 5 p.m. Is it possible to schedule an interview during these times? If not, I would be happy to find a **time that is convenient for both of us**（我們都方便的時間）.

I am excited to learn more about the opportunities at Hotel Comfy and look forward to discussing the role in greater detail. Please let me know if there is any additional information you would like for me to provide or if there are any documents or certificates you would like me to bring on the day of the interview. Thanks!

Yours sincerely,

Charlene Fong

Phone: (+852) 9123-4567

回應面試邀請電郵範例（三）

Dear Ms. Lam,

I am **thrilled**（激動／高興）to have the opportunity to interview for the **Junior Graphic Designer**（初級圖形設計師）position at Ideal Collection. It is my **career goal**（職業目標）at present to work with a major manufacturer like Ideal, which has a wide variety of household and other products.

Yes, I am available for an interview at 10:00 a.m. Tuesday. As for work **samples**（樣本）, I have my own **portfolio**（作品集）which displays all my work on many different consumer products. You can take a look at my ability to use color and image mixes.

Besides, I am attaching in this email an updated copy of my resume that includes a new product which I designed recently. The work includes a combination of **package design**（包裝設計）, **in-store signage**（店內品牌）, and Internet advertising. I will be sure to add samples from the project to my portfolio.

Please let me know if there is anything else I have to bring. Thank you again for the chance to interview. I look forward to meeting you.

Yours sincerely,

David Li

9123-4567 (cell)

3.2 透過電話回覆面試邀請

接電話時，記得控制說話的語氣以及音調，
嘗試透過聲浪表現出自己的熱情。

1-3.2-01

實用句式 1

Thank you for your invitation to interview with (company name). Yes, I am available at (time) on (date).

感謝　貴公司給予我面試的機會。是的，我於（日期）（時間）能前來（公司名稱）參與面試。

例句

Thank you for your invitation to interview with Z & Y Collection. Yes, I am available at 10:30 am on 30th May, 2021.

感謝貴公司給予我面試的機會。是的，我於 2021 年 5 月 30 日上午 10:30 能前來參與面試。

實用句式 2

Thank you so much for reaching out to me. Yes, I am available at (time) on (date).

非常感謝您與我聯繫。是的,我在(日期)的(時間)有空。

例句

Thank you so much for reaching out to me. Yes, I am available at 11am on this Friday.

非常感謝您與我聯繫。是的,這個星期五上午 11 時有空。

假如你因有事而不能如約參加面試,語氣中記得帶歉意,並且要積極、主動地和對方商議另選時間,以免錯失寶貴的面試機會。

1-3.2-02

實用句式 1

Hello, (Caller's name). I appreciate the opportunity to interview with (Company Name). Unfortunately, I'm not available at the time you proposed. Would you be available (Your Availability) instead?

你好,(來電者姓名)。我很高興有機會參與(公司名稱)的面試。很抱歉,您提出的面試時間我剛好沒空。或者,您 _____ 有空嗎?

Hello, Mr Chan. I appreciate the opportunity to interview with L & Y Collection. Unfortunately, I'm not available at the time you proposed. Would you be available after 1:00 p.m. on that day instead?

你好，陳先生。我很高興有機會參與 L & Y Collection 的面試。很抱歉，您提出的面試時間我剛好沒空。或者，您當天下午 1:00 後有空嗎？

實用句式 2

If not, I would be happy to find a time that is convenient for both of us.

如果不行的話，我很樂意找一個我們都方便的時間。

實用句式 3

I apologize for causing any inconvenience, but I'm really enthusiastic about this opportunity and I hope that you can reschedule this interview.

對於給您帶來的任何不便，我深表歉意，但是我對這個機會非常熱衷，希望您能重新安排這次面試的時間。

如果不小心錯過了對方的來電，記得檢查一下有沒有收到任何口訊，對方很有可能會在留言訊息中告知你他的聯絡電話以及辦公時間。致電對方時，你可以説：

■ 實用句子

Thank you for calling to schedule an interview time. I'm sorry I wasn't able to take your call, but I'm available to interview with you on (date) at (time) to discuss this position in more detail.

感謝您致電安排面試時間。很抱歉，我剛剛無法接聽您的電話。我可以在（日期）（時間）與您面談，以更詳細地討論這職位。

例句

Thank you for calling to schedule an interview time. I'm sorry I wasn't able to take your call, but I'm available to interview with you on 3rd April at 9 a.m. to discuss this position in more detail.

感謝您致電安排面試時間。很抱歉，我剛剛無法接聽您的電話。我可以在 4 月 3 日上午 9 時與您面談，以更詳細地討論這職位。

Appendix 2 / Appendix 1 / Part 2

Part 1

求職相關的問題

電話回覆面試邀請對答範例

1-3.2-04

Mandy: Hello, Miss Lam. This is Mandy Choi, and I am **returning your call**（回電）to schedule a phone interview for the **Junior Sales Executive**（初級銷售代表）position.

HR manager: Hi, Mandy. **Thanks for returning my call**（感謝您回電）. You can call me Kathy. I'm the HR manager of Z & Y Fashion.

Mandy: Nice to meet you, Kathy.

HR manager: As mentioned in the voice message I left you, having taken a look at your C.V., and **given the kind of outgoing**（外向的）and **enthusiastic**（熱情的）person you are, we'd like to invite you for an interview on this Thursday at 10 am. Are you available at that time?

Mandy: Yes, 10 am on Thursday is perfect for me.

HR manager: Great. So I'll put you in for 10 am on this Thursday.

Mandy: Yes, that would be great. Thank you. By the way, do I have to bring any additional documents?

HR manager. Yes, please bring along your **official academic transcripts**（成績表）and **certificates**（證書）on that day.

Mandy: No problem. Thanks！

HR manager: Have a nice day. Good-bye.

Mandy: Thanks. Good-bye.

小貼士

1 別忘了查閱垃圾郵件信箱

發出求職電郵後，記得每天也要反覆查閱收件箱，以免忽略了對方的任何通知。有時候，重要的郵件也會莫名其妙地跑到"junk mail folder / spam folder（垃圾郵件信箱）"裏，因此，查閱郵箱的時候，記得順便查看垃圾郵件郵箱，以免錯過重要郵件。

2 收到郵件通知後要及時回覆

收到面試通知後，切記及時回覆對方，以免給人一種錯覺你已經找到另一份心儀的工作，或已經改變注意，不再希望應徵本來申請的職位。如果有這樣的誤會，對方就有可能另覓面試的人選，導致你失去面試的機會了。相信你也不想收到這樣的訊息吧：

求職相關的問題

We have been waiting for you for whole day, but still haven't received your email reply. We think you are not interested in our company or you have found another job. Therefore, when we have already notified another job applicant to come to our company for an interview.

我們已經等了你一天了，但仍沒有收到你的郵件回覆，因此，我們以為你對本公司不感興趣或者你已經找到了合適的工作。於是，我們已經通知了另外一位求職者來我們公司面試了。

3.3 透過電話回覆視像面試（Video interview）

現今 Video interview（視像面試）招聘模式越來越普及。隨着科技進步以及各種因素（如疫情肆虐），很多公司已習慣把面試改為在線上進行，透過用 Zoom、Microsoft Teams、Skype 等平台進行。

範例

對答範例

1-3.3-01

HR manager: Hello. Is this Peter Wong?
Peter: Yes, I am.

HR manager: Hello Peter. My name is Candy, the HR manager of ABC Education Center. Thank you for your interest for our Teaching Assistant position. We'd like to invite you for an interview. However, due to the current COVID-19 situation, our interviews have to be conducted online. Therefore, we'd like to invite you for a Zoom interview to get to know you better. Are you available on this Friday?

Peter: Thank you so much for reaching out to me. Yes, I'm available on this Friday.

HR manager: Great. How about 2pm?

Peter: No problem. I'm available anytime on this Friday.

HR manager: Okay. Our team leader Jason Lam will meet you on Zoom on this Friday. A **^Zoom invitation link** will be sent to you by email two days before your interview. May I have your email address, please?

^ 登入 Zoom 後，只需前往邀請網址（i.e. invitation link），就可以加入視訊會議。

Peter: Sure. My email address is peterwong@email.com.

HR manager: p-e-t-e-r-w-o-n-g@email.com. Right?

求職相關的問題

Peter:　　　　Yes.

HR manager: Okay. Please check your email on this Wednesday. We'll send you the invitation link in the morning. Also, you can contact me at 2123-4567 if you encounter any issues on the day.

Peter:　　　　Thanks again! I'm looking forward to discussing the role with Mr. Lam on this Friday.

HR manager: Have a nice day. Good-bye.

Peter:　　　　Thanks. Good-bye.

小貼士

關於 Video interview（視像面試）

進行 Video interview（視像面試）之前，記得提前準備好畢業證書、工作證明等重要文件。

一般而言，在 face-to-face 的面試中，公司都會要求求職者帶上履歷表 (C.V.)、成績表 (official academic transcripts)、證書 (certificates) 以及其他證明文件等的正本或影印本，證明自己的學歷和工作經驗。然而，在 Video interview 時，很多求職者都會忘記了提前把這些文件放置於電腦附近，導致當對方要求查看相關文件的時候，才「臨急臨忙」跑去拿資料，顯得極度不專業。

求職英語一本通

Question

Tell me a little about yourself.
請簡單介紹一下你自己。

1-4-01

其他類似問法

What kinds of skills do you have?

你有甚麼技能？

Tell me about your personalities.

告訴我你的性格。

面試官問你這問題的原因是為了更了解你的性格和興趣，從而判斷你是否適合的人選。當回答這道問題時，謹記保持誠實，並簡單描述一下自己的個性（personalities）、特質（attributes）、天賦（talents）。此外，不應提及一些無關緊要的內容，也不要說太多有關個人生活的細節。

■ 可提及的內容

📌 Skills and / or qualities relevant to the position
與職位相關的技能和 / 或特質

📌 Prior experience
以往的經驗

📌 Your career goals
你的職業目標

■ 不應提及的內容

📌 Skills and / or qualities irrelevant to the position
與職位無關的技能和 / 或特質

📌 Irrelevant personal information
不相關的個人訊息

📌 Unprofessional attributes
不專業的個人特質

1-4-02

有關個性（personalities）的形容詞 (adj.)

Active	積極的；行動派的
Ambitious	雄心勃勃
Analytical	分析型的
Adaptable	適應性強的
Alert	機警的

Capable（+of）	有能力的
Creative	富創意的
Cooperative	合作的
Conscientious	認真的；盡責的
Dependable	可靠的
Detail-oriented	做事謹慎的
Diligent	勤奮的
Down-to-earth	腳踏實地的
Easy-going	隨和的
Efficient	有效率的
Flexible	懂變通的
Generous	慷慨的
Goal-oriented	目標導向的
Helpful	樂於助人的
Innovative	有創意的
Kind	親切的
Mature	成熟的
Methodical	有條不紊的；井井有條的；循序漸進的
Objective	客觀的
Optimistic	樂觀的

Outgoing	外向的
Patient	有耐心的
Punctual	守時的
Reliable	可靠的
Result-oriented	重結果的
Sociable	好交際的
Vibrant	精力充沛的
Wise	明智的

當你形容完自己之後，加一個 Example 就可以延長句子以及加深對方的印象。

1-4-03

■ 簡短回答

🔖 I am an innovative designer with over 6 years experience creating unique exhibitions.

我是一位創新設計師，並擁有超過 6 年創作獨特展覽的經驗。

🔖 I'm pretty conscientious; I take my duties very seriously.

我很盡職；我非常重視我的職責。

📌 I'm quite easy-going. I always collaborate happily with colleagues to get the projects done.

我很隨和，而且總能愉快地與同事合作完成項目。

📌 I'm a very reliable person; you can surely depend on me to get your tasks done on time.

我是一個非常可靠的人。您可以放心依靠我按時完成你分配的工作。

📌 I'm a methodical person; I take care of my work well.

我是一個很有條理的人，我能好好處理工作的。

📌 I'm a very diligent person. I make sure to put in all my efforts to accomplish my tasks.

我是一個非常勤奮的人，我確保自己能盡我所有的努力來完成各項任務。

📌 I'm an analytical problem solver with a creative edge and a passion for technology, innovation and people.

我是一個分析型問題解決者，具有創造力，對技術、創新和人員充滿熱情。

求職相關的問題

有關「特質 (attributes)」的描述

e.g. I'm a decision maker.	我是一位決策者
A decision maker	決策者
An efficient worker	有效率的員工
A good listener	好聽眾
A great team player	很好的團隊工作者
A hard worker	努力工作的人
A result-getter	成果達成者
A self-starter	自發的、自動自覺的人
A quick learner	領悟力高的人
A good fit	合適的人

有關「技能 (skills)」的動詞 (v.)

administer (v.) 處理 / 管理

e.g. I am trained to work under high pressure in a fast-paced environment and work independently within a team. I can also administer several cases simultaneously within the requisite time frames.

我能在節奏急速的環境中和壓力底下工作,並在團隊中獨立工作。此外,我也能夠在有限的時間內同時處理多個工作。

advise (v.) 提出建議

e.g. I am capable of advising clients in terms of their investments, retirement, estate, debt and savings management.

我有能力為客戶提供投資、退休、房地產、債務和儲蓄管理方面的建議。

evaluate (v.) 評估

e.g. I am able to evaluate a software design at the component level and from the perspective of software reuse.

我能夠從組件級別並從軟件重用的角度評估軟件設計。

Appendix 2　Appendix 1　Part 2

Part 1

求職相關的問題

identify (v.) 辨識

e.g. I am good at identifying the needs of clients. My goal is making people's dream come true in the field of real estate.

我擅長辨識客戶的需求,我的目標是在房地產領域實現人們的夢想。

initiate (v.) 創設

e.g. I have initiated a software development project to automate the current working process for a more efficient workflow.

我已經啟動了一個軟件開發項目,使當前的工作流程自動化,以實現更高效的工作流程。

plan (v.) 策劃

e.g. I am good at planning and organizing things and will use all my potential to fulfil the same in this industry.

我擅長計劃和組織事物,並會盡我所能來實現這一行業中的目標。

negotiate (v.) 協商談判

e.g. I am good at negotiating and closing sales.

我擅長談判和達成交易。

1-4-06

■ 必學句型

📌 I graduated from（學校名稱）with a（學位名稱；e.g. Bachelor's degree in Information Technology).

我畢業於 _____，並擁有 _____ 學位。

📌 I'm ready to begin my career in the（部門名稱；e.g. Information Technology) division of a successful company.

我準備在一家成功的公司的 _____ 部門開始我的職業生涯。

📌 I am experienced in _____（e.g. computer programming and data system).

我有 _____ 的經驗。

📌 I'm a _____ person who _____（e.g. can be successful to help develop the new market by utilizing my marketing and language skills).

我是一個 _____ 的人。我可 _____。

📌 I am confident that _____.

我有信心 _____。

參考回答範例

1-4-07

〔先說明自己在這個行業打滾了多久〕**I have been working in the** customer service（客戶服務）**industry for** over seven years.

我已經在客戶服務行業工作了 7 年以上。

〔然後談及相關經驗〕：**My most recent experience has been** handling client's phone calls（處理客戶的電話）. One reason I particularly enjoy this business is the opportunity to connect with people. **In my previous role as** a customer service officer, I formed some significant customer relationships（客戶關係）, which resulted in a 25 percent increase in sales（銷售額增長）in a matter of months.

我最近的經驗是處理客戶的電話。我特別喜歡這項業務的原因之一是有機會與人們建立聯繫。在擔任客戶服務主任之前，我建立了一些重要的客戶關係，在短短幾個月內使銷售額增長了 25％。

〔說明自己的性格、特質〕：**My real strength** is my attention to detail. I'm a methodical（有條不紊的）and conscientious（認真負責的）person, and I pride myself on my reputation（聲譽）for meeting deadlines. When I commit to doing something, I make sure it gets done on time.

我真正的長處是對細節的關注。我是一個有條不紊及認真負責的人，我很自豪自己總能在限期前完成任務，並在這方面有良好的聲譽──當我承諾做某件事時，我確保它按時完成。

What I am looking for now is a company that values customer relations, where I can join a strong team and have a positive impact on customer retention and sales.

我現正尋找一家重視客戶關係的公司，讓我可以加入一支強大的團隊，並對保留客戶和銷售產生積極影響。

求職相關的問題

小貼士

請記住，面試需要有專業的舉止。即使面試是在 Zoom、Skype 等網絡平台上進行，你也必須表現出專業精神。

Video interview（視像面試）要注意甚麼？

1. Look into the camera while speaking 説話時看着鏡頭。

2. 視像面試中，別忘了與面試官保持眼神交流，因為這可以表明你尊重他，並凸顯出自己的信心。面試前，記得檢查一下攝像頭，如果畫面不清，可能要清潔鏡頭。此外，記得檢查鏡頭角度，切忌「高炒」或「低炒」。

3. 面試時，不論屏幕上出現多少個人，你的眼神也應直視鏡頭，不要將焦點放在自己的儀容上，否則會給對方「分神」的感覺。因此，面試開始前記得先整理好儀容。要讓面試官有眼神交流的感覺，記得在交流的過程中望着鏡頭。

在正式面試之前，僱主或 HR 只能透過閱覽求職者的求職信以及履歷表等資料，間接了解求職者的背景，然而，單憑藉一份完美的求職信和履歷表只能助你取得與僱主或 HR 見面的「入場券」，離正式獲得聘用這「終極目標」還遠着呢！是否能拿下心儀的職位空缺、順利入職新公司的關鍵，其實更在於你是否能把握面試機會，在短短的會面時間中在僱主或 HR 面前施盡渾身解數、好好表現自己。

面試時間沒有特定的長短或時限，取決個別公司或企業的決定，另外也有可能視乎情況，按個別需要而定。然而，普遍來說，由於僱主或 HR 大多都公事繁忙，而於面試當日或許還需面見眾多的求職者，所以面見每個求職者的時間一般不會太長。如果你想在有限的面試時間當中讓僱主或 HR 對你另眼相看的話，就必須學會在短時間內表現出過人之處，促使對方認同你的能力，並相信你是有關職位的不二人選。

在這個單元中，筆者會為你介紹一系列的面試問題，當中，每一類別包含兩組到五組問題，並提供 "Useful words & expressions"、「必學句型」、「簡短回答」及「參考回答範例」。你也可以掃描旁邊的 QR code 來聽聽說話者說話的語調、語速和發音，並嘗試自己唸一次，參考回答範例及詞彙，繼而試着用自己的方式來回答每一道問題。這個部分只要多加練習，面試時就能從容不迫、得心應手，把自己最好的一面呈現出來。

5.1 類別（1）：應聘這份工作的原因

「你為甚麼會想應聘這份工作？」是面試中一道極為常見的問題。在僱主或 HR 的角度而言，出發點是為着初步了解面試者的求職意欲從何而來，並進一步了解面試者於甚麼原因應聘這一份工作。他們可以根據你的回答，初探你的職業目標，並以此作為依據，初步衡量你是否任職有關職位合適的人選。除此以外，這類問題亦有助於他們測試面試者對有關職位的認知，並對這份工作有多感興趣，進而窺探對入職該職位是否抱有足夠的誠意和熱忱。

回答這一類問題並沒有一套既定的方法，也沒有所謂「滿分」的答案，你的回覆其實有很大的發揮空間，內容也富有很大的彈性。面對這種提問，你只需保持鎮定，並以滿足面試人員發問的目的為由，坦誠告知對方自己申請入職該職位的原因即可。

內容方面，你可以綜合自己的心路歷程以及個人的歷練，自行選材、組織、發揮。你既可交代有關職位吸引你的地方，也可說明自己為何是一個合適的入職人選。當然，你必須回答得大方得體，內容也應合乎邏輯，這樣才可讓對方感覺到你是個談吐得宜、懂得禮節，而且思路清晰、具有條理的人。

那麼，我們又可以怎麼透過回覆的內容凸顯自己應聘的誠意呢？筆者建議大家不妨在參與面試之前做好事前的「功課」，查明公司以及有關職位的資料，多了解該公司的理念以及有關職位的一些具體的學歷或資歷要求。在做好準備工夫、資料俱備的情況下，我們不但能更輕易準備讓對方滿意的答案，也可憑藉自己對公司以及有關職位的了解，表現自己應聘的誠意和決心。

Question 1

Why did you apply for this job?
你為何申請這個職位？

1-5.1-01

其他類似問法

Why are you interested in this role?

你為甚麼對這個職位感興趣？

Describe why you are interested in this position.

描述一下你為甚麼對這個職位感興趣。

What made you interested in applying for this position?

你為甚麼對這個職位感興趣？

Why do you want to work here?

你為甚麼想在這裏工作？

1-5.1-02

Useful words & expressions

be a good fit for...... (v phr.)	對⋯⋯來說合適
an ideal job (n phr.)	理想的工作
be drawn to this job (v phr.)	被這工作吸引
company reputation (n phr.)	公司的聲譽
reputation of key leaders (n phr.)	公司主要領導者的聲譽
admiration of products/ services (n phr.)	對產品或服務的欣賞
admiration of training programs (n phr.)	對培訓課程的欣賞
company culture and values (n phr.)	公司文化和價值觀

company growth (n phr.)	公司成長
on the rise (prep phr.)	正在崛起
be eager to…… (v phr.)	渴望
mission (n.)	使命

1-5.1-03

■ 必學句型

🖈 This job is a good fit for my background in _____.
這份工作與我的 _____ 背景相符。

🖈 I would be proud to build a career with (company's name).
我為在　貴公司建立事業而感到自豪。

🖈 I consider myself _____ and it would be great if I can work for a company that's _____.
我認為自己是 _____，如果我能在 _____ 的公司工作，那就太好了。

🖈 This position is _____ in my career.
這份工作是我職業規劃中 _____ 的一部分。

Working in this company would give me the opportunity to build upon my experience and skills in _____ (e.g. financial services) as part of what I know would be a really inspiring and rewarding environment, based upon what I've heard about your company.

在這家公司工作將使我有機會在 _____ （e.g. 金融服務）方面積累經驗和技能。根據我對　貴公司的了解，我知道這將是一個非常鼓舞人心和收穫豐富的環境。

簡短回答

This job is a good fit for my background in marketing.

這份工作與我的市場營銷背景相符。

1-5.1-04

I would be proud to build a career with L&Y Collection LTD.

我為在 L&Y Collection LTD 建立事業而感到自豪。

I consider myself an innovator and it would be great if I can work for a company that's leading the future of the industry.

我認為自己是個創新者，如果我可以在能領導行業未來的公司工作，那就太好了。

This position is logical in my career.

這份工作是我職業規劃中合理的一步。

範例

參考回答範例（一）

1-5.1-05

I understand that this is a company that is **on the rise**（正在崛起）. As I've read on your website, I know that you're planning to launch a series of new products in the coming season. I'm **eager**（我渴望）to be a part of this business as it grows, and I'm confident that my experience in product development would help your company as you **roll out**（推出）these products. Indeed, I'd be proud to build a career with you.

我知道這是一家正在崛起的公司。正如我在您的網站上所讀到的，我知道　貴公司計劃在下季節推出一系列新產品。我渴望能參與並一同發展這個計劃。我有信心我在產品開發方面的經驗將為　貴公司推出這些產品提供幫助。説真的，倘若我能在　貴公司工作，我定必感到自豪。

I have been admiring your company's successful strategies and **mission**（使命）since 2016. Your emphasis on creating a strong relationship between your company and the surrounding community have brought you success everywhere you have opened an office. In fact, these are the values I greatly admire. That's why I was **drawn to this job**（被這工作吸引）. I'm eager to make contributions, and this position is **a good fit for**（對……來說合適）my background and your needs.

自 2016 年以來，我一直非常欣賞　貴公司成功的策略和使命。　貴公司一直重視與周圍社區之間建立良好關係的重要性，從而使公司在所有開設了辦事處的地方都獲得了成功。實際上，這些都是我非常佩服的價值觀，這就是我被這份工作所吸引之原因。我渴望為公司作出貢獻，而這個職位也與我的背景和您的需求相符。

小貼士

1 不要提供過於籠統（general）的答案

錯誤示範

This is a great company and I'd like to work here.

這是一家很棒的公司，我想在這裏工作。

（此回答過於籠統，而非僅適用於此職位，因而給人一種沒有做資料搜集的感覺。）

2 切忌讓對方感到您沒有誠意

錯誤示範

I heard there were some open positions, so here I am.

我聽説這裏有一些空缺職位，所以我來了。

（此回答給人一種過於被動的感覺。）

Why do you think you are the best candidate for this position?

1-5.1-07

為甚麼你認為你是這個職位 的最佳人選？

面試前，記得確保自己已經仔細閱讀了求職廣告中的「職 位描述 (job description)」，以準確了解公司的需求，並細 閱自己的 C.V.、過去的經驗和技能。

其他類似問法

Why should we hire you?

我們為甚麼要僱用你？

Why are you the best person for this job?

為甚麼你是這份工作的最佳人選？

What would you bring to this position?

你會為公司帶來甚麼？

Why do you think you are the right fit for this role?

為甚麼你認為自己適合這個職位？

Useful words & expressions

be an excellent fit (v phr.)	對……來説非常合適
an attitude for excellence (n phr.)	追求卓越的態度
an infectious desire (n phr.)	極強的感染力
highly motivated (adj.)	積極進取的
result-oriented (adj.)	重視結果的
to go an extra mile (v phr.)	付出更多的努力
to surpass (v.)	超越
better means (n phr.)	更佳的方法
to thrive (v.)	蓬勃發展
be well acquainted with sth. (v phr.)	熟悉（某事）
be passionate about sth. (v phr.)	對（某事）充滿熱情
be applicable for this role (v phr.)	適用於此職位
to grow your business (v phr.)	發展你的業務
the best match for this position (n phr.)	此職位的最佳人選
my top priority (n phr.)	我的首要任務；我的重中之重
to multitask (v.)	同時處理多個任務
to spread my wings (v phr.)	展翅高飛

■ 必學句型

🎈 I believe I'm an excellent fit with (company's name).
我相信自己非常適合　貴公司。

🎈 My education and my previous job working as
_____ for_____ (company's name)
provided me with the ideal experience for this position.
我的學歷背景和曾於 _____ 公司擔任 _____
的經驗為我提供了擔任這職位的理想經驗。

🎈 I look forward to contributing my _____ skills
and experiences to your organization.
我期待着將我的 _____ 技能和經驗貢獻給　貴公司。

🎈 I know _____ inside out.
我對 _____ 瞭如指掌。

1-5.1-10

■ 簡短回答

🎈 I believe I'm an excellent fit with L & Y Collection LTD.
我相信我非常適合 L & Y Collection LTD。

🎈 My education and my previous job working as an
editor for L & Y magazine provided me with the ideal
experience for this position.
我的學歷背景和曾於 L & Y 公司擔任雜誌編輯的經驗為
我提供了擔任這職位的理想經驗。

🖈 I look forward to contributing my programming skills to L & Y company so as to make our mobile App(lication) accessible to everyone.

我希望為 L & Y 公司貢獻自己的編程技能，以使每個人都可以使用　貴公司的手機應用程式。

🖈 I know the local market inside out.

我對本地市場瞭如指掌。

範例

參考回答範例

1-5.1-11

I believe I'm an **excellent fit**（非常適合） with your company. There may be others with similar abilities, but I have something they may not have. I have an **attitude for excellence**（追求卓越的態度）, and **an infectious desire**（極強的感染力）to participate in shaping organizational change. Besides, I am **a highly motivated**（積極進取）, **result-oriented**（重視結果）individual, who is **willing to go an extra mile**（付出更多的努力）to reach goals and learn along the way. For example, my previous job involved meeting specific targets on a daily basis, which I managed and sometimes **surpassed**（超越）while **gaining better means**（更佳的方法）of improving the achievement of those goals. I'm confident that if given this opportunity,

求職相關的問題

I will **thrive**（蓬勃發展）and deliver quality work **within stipulated deadlines**（規定的期限內）. I look forward to contributing my skills and experiences to your organization.

我相信自己非常適合　貴公司。或許其他人也具有類似的能力，但我擁有一些他們可能沒有的才能——追求卓越的態度和極強的感染力。因此，我渴望能一同參與組織變革。此外，我是一個積極進取、重視結果的人，我願意付出更多的努力來達成目標並持續學習。例如，我上一份工作要求員工每天達成特定的目標，我也會設法處理好每一個項目，間中甚至會超越預設的目標，同時得出實現這些目標更佳的方法。我相信，如果有幸於貴公司工作，我一定會蓬勃發展，並在規定的期限內完成高質量的工作。我期待着將我的技能和經驗貢獻給您們。

小貼士

説「我不知道」或給出模糊的答案絕不是回答任何面試問題的好方法。如有需要，請花點時間思考一下再回答。你也可以先從自己的資歷和能力開始，告知對方你如何能勝任這份工作，並附帶一些軼事或過去的經驗來説明。

參考示例

A: Why should we hire you?

B:〔先從自己的資歷和能力開始〕My background experience, as a sales representative, equipped me with the relevant skills for this role. I'm very ambitious and determined to achieve my goals, and my enthusiasm to get work done motivates my team members.

〔附帶一些軼事或過去的經驗來說明〕In the past six months, my team and I were ranked among the top five sales teams in the industry......

5.2 類別（2）：學歷背景及工作經歷

Question 1

What did you learn from your (previous job / degree)？

你從（上一份工作／你的學位）中學到甚麼？

1-5.2-01

What did you learn in your last job?

你從上一份工作學到甚麼？

What have you learned from your past experience or your last job?

你從過去的經驗中或是上一個工作裏，學到了甚麼？

What did you learn from your degree?

你從你的學位中學到了甚麼？

What did you learn in college?

你在大學裏學到了甚麼？

"What did you learn from your previous job / degree？"是面試官經常詢問求職者的問題，目的是了解求職者的領悟力和執行力。

站在上司和僱主的立場，他們當然希望可以聘請到一個悟性高的員工，好讓他們在執行大小事務時都能省心省力。因此，對方希望看看應徵者是否能總結自己過去的努力，同時確認他們是否清楚自己的職涯發展目標。

Useful words & expressions

academic (adj.)	學術的
practical skills (n phr.)	實用的技能
communication skills (n phr.)	溝通技巧
written skills (n phr.)	寫作技巧
to communicate effectively (v phr.)	有效溝通
to deal with (v phr.)	處理
to edit (v.)	編輯
to provide feedback (v phr.)	提供意見 / 反饋
productive (adj.)	富有成效的
be responsible for (v phr.)	負責

1-5.2-03

必學句型

📌 My _____ degree gave me a range of academic and practical skills, especially _____ skills.

我的 _____ 學位為我提供了一系列的學術和實用的技能，尤其是 _____ 技能。

求職相關的問題

139

Other skills that have helped me in the job include
_____ .

對我工作有幫助的其他技能包括 _____。

My previous job involved _____ .
我以前的工作涉及 _____。

In my previous role as a/an _____ , I always had
to _____ .
以前當我擔任 _____ 時，我總 _____。

Thanks to this invaluable experience, I _____ .
正正因為這些寶貴的經驗，我學會了 _____。

1-5.2-04

簡短回答

My Bachelor's in Education degree gave me a
range of academic and practical skills, especially
communication and written skills.

我的教育學士學位為我提供了一系列的學術和實用的技
能，尤其是針對溝通和寫作技能。

Other skills that have helped me in the job include verbal
skills, problem solving skills, time management skills
and adaptability.

現在，我可以在與學生合作時將其付諸實踐。對我工作
有幫助的其他技能包括口頭表達能力、解難能力、時間
管理能力和適應力。

📌 In my previous role as a customer service assistant, I always had to work under pressure.

以前當我擔任客戶服務助理時，我總在壓力下工作。

📌 Thanks to this invaluable experience, I feel I have become a better worker who is able to handle a number of tasks concurrently.

正正因為這些寶貴的經驗，我學會了同時處理多項任務，也使我成為了一名更好的員工。

範例

參考回答範例（一）

1-5.2-05

My Bachelor's in Education degree gave me a range of academic and practical skills, especially communication and written skills. Now, I am able to put this into practice when working with my students. Other skills that have helped me in the job include verbal skills, problem solving skills, time management skills and adaptability.

我的教育學士學位為我提供了一系列的學術和實踐技能，尤其是針對溝通和寫作技能。現在，我可以在與學生合作時將其付諸實踐。對我工作有幫助的其他技能包括口頭表達能力、解難能力、時間管理能力和適應力。

求職相關的問題

參考回答範例（二）

1-5.2-06

My previous job involved meeting specific targets on a daily basis, which I managed and sometimes surpassed while gaining better means of improving the achievement of those goals. I'm confident that if given this opportunity, I will thrive and deliver quality work within stipulated deadlines. I look forward to contributing my skills and experiences to your organization.

我以前的工作涉及每天實現特定目標。我需要設法管理，有時甚至超出預期目標。同時，我也獲得了改善實現這些目標的更好方法。我相信如果有這個機會在你公司工作，我會蓬勃發展並在規定的期限內完成高質量的工作。我期待着將我的技能和經驗貢獻給　貴公司。

範例

參考回答範例（三）

1-5.2-07

In my previous role as a **customer service assistant**（客戶服務助理）, I always had to work under pressure. **Thanks to**（得益於／基於／多得）this invaluable experience, I feel I have become a better worker who is able to handle a number of tasks

concurrently（同時地）. When I had to deal with several unsatisfied customers, I would focus on the task at hand rather than feeling stressed. I believe that my ability to communicate effectively with customers helps reduce my own stress as well as any stress the customer may feel.

以前當我擔任客戶服務助理時，壓力無處不在。但也正正因為這些寶貴的經驗，我學會了同時處理多項任務，也使我成為了一名更好的員工。每當我需要同時處理一些比較棘手的顧客時，我都會專注於當前的任務而非其壓力。我相信與客戶溝通的能力有助於減輕我的壓力以及安撫客戶，問題也變得更加容易處理。

範例

參考回答範例（四）

1-5.2-08

In my previous role as an office assistant, sometimes I had to edit my team member's work and provide feedback for areas of improvement. Through this experience, I realized that feedback can be both helpful and kind, when delivered the right way. Since then, I've become better at offering feedback, and I've realized that my empathy can be used to my advantage to provide thoughtful and productive feedback.

在上一份工作，作為辦公室助理的我間中也需編輯團隊成員的工作成果，並提供意見以供改進。這經驗不但讓我獲益良多，同時也讓我意識到以正確的方式給予他人意見的好處——既可表示友好，亦能達到相得益彰之效。自此，我更樂於予人意見，而這方面的能力亦隨之竿頭直上。與此同時，我亦意識到原來自己可運用同理心去為他人提供具建設性的意見，從而發揮我的優勢。

範例

參考回答範例（五）

In my previous role as a Marketing Assistant, I had to help initiate a series of marketing campaigns including print, digital, and social media analysis, and content for direct mail campaigns.

在上一份工作，作為市場營銷助理的我負責市場營銷活動，包括印刷版、電子版和分析社交媒體，以及郵件促銷。

參考回答範例（六）

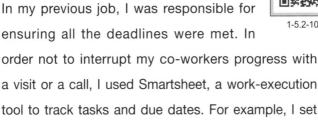

1-5.2-10

In my previous job, I was responsible for ensuring all the deadlines were met. In order not to interrupt my co-workers progress with a visit or a call, I used Smartsheet, a work-execution tool to track tasks and due dates. For example, I set alerts, updates, and reminders for them.

在上一份工作中，我負責確保工作都在限期內完成。為了不打斷同事的工作，我使用了工作表執行工具 Smartsheet 來觀察任務的進度和到期日。例如，我為它們設置了預報、更新和提醒。

5.3 類別（3）：個人特質及能力

Question 1

Do you prefer working in a team environment or by yourself？

你喜歡在團隊環境中工作還是獨自工作？

1-5.3-01

Do you prefer working independently or on a team?

你喜歡獨自工作還是團隊合作？

Would you rather work on a team or alone?

你傾向喜歡與團隊一起工作還是自己一個人工作？

How do you feel about working in a team environment?

你在團隊環境中工作的感覺如何？

How do you feel about working individually?

你對獨自工作有何感想？

"Do you prefer working in a team environment or by yourself?" 這個問題之所以棘手，是因為確實沒有一個「正確」的答案。歸根結底，面試官之所以詢問應徵者傾向喜歡團隊合作還是個人工作，是希望了解對方是內向還是外向的人。

性格外向的人喜歡與他人共事，並且在與同時合作時會充滿活力。另一方面，性格內向的人渴望能在安靜的環境下在獨自工作。然而，實際上，團隊合作和個人合作都有積極和消極的一面。

假如你的回應是："I prefer working in a team environment."
的話，面試官可能會誤解你需要其他人的意見和建議才
能做出決定。他們可能會認為與團隊合作是幫助你完成
自己的工作的一種方式。而且，如果你要申請遠程工作
（a remote job），那麼，這將對您不利，因為遠程工作大
多要求員工獨立工作。

可是，假如你的回應是："I prefer working alone."的話，
面試官可能會誤解你不太願意與同事交流。

那麼，我們到底該如何回答此問題呢？如何回答才能將
"teamwork" 與 "individual work" 的好處結合起來呢？

小貼士

技巧

你可以先提及自己的偏好，並說明自己很彈性
（Flexible），兩種模式也能適應（如果的確如此）。這意
味着雖然你喜歡團隊環境，但是你也可以獨立工作的。

Useful words & expressions

beneficial (adj.)	有利的;有益的
a team player (n phr.)	團隊成員
cooperative (ad.)	合作的
open-minded (adj.)	思想開明的
to feel more motivated (v phr.)	更有動力
to congregate together (v phr.)	聚集在一起
to come up with a completely new creative thought or idea (v phr.)	提出一個全新的、具創意的思想或想法
to work independently (v phr.)	當我獨立工作時
to focus much better on the task at hand (v phr.)	更好地專注於手頭上的任務
to formulate my thoughts well (v phr.)	順利地構思我的想法

必學句型

It depends on……
這取決於……

1-5.3-03

I am able to …… , but I do enjoy ……
我有能力 …… 但是我也很喜歡 ……

Based on my personal experience, I found that ……
根據我的個人經驗 ……

According to the job description, the right job candidate should …… . That very much fits with the way I do my best work, too.
根據職位描述，求職者應該 ……。這工作方式非常適合我。

When it comes to brainstorming, I believe that ……
在集思廣益方面，我相信 ……

1-5.3-04

簡短回答

Actually, I enjoy both. I am able to work both on a team and work alone.
實際上我都喜歡。我既可以團隊合作，也可以獨自工作。

It depends on the project that needs to be done.
這取決於需要完成的項目。

I am able to work individually to complete the tasks on time（按時）, but I do enjoy brainstorming（集思廣益）and collaborating（合作）with my teammates.
我可以單獨工作以按時完成任務，但是我也很喜歡與隊友合作並集思廣益。

求職相關的問題

📌 Based on my personal experience, I found that having multiple（多個）brains working toward the same final product was indeed（確實）beneficial.

根據我的個人經驗，我發現大家共同致力於鑽研同一產品確實是很有效的。

📌 I have the ability to work in a team setting and independently to meet team goals（團隊目標）.

我有能力在團隊合作中獨立工作，以實現團隊目標。

📌 I have immensely enjoyed playing both roles（同時扮演兩個角色）, and I think that I would be comfortable in both roles, that of a team member as well as a sole entity（獨立個體）.

我非常享受同時扮演兩個角色──作為一個團隊成員和獨立個體。我覺得兩個角色對我而言都相當輕鬆。

此外，面試前記得細閱職位描述（Job Description），當被問到這問題時，你就可以引用其作為答案的一部分。

例子

Job Description：
- Ability to establish priorities, work independently（獨立工作）, and proceed with objectives without supervision（沒有監督的情況下）.
- Excellent attention to detail
- Well-organized and able to handle pressure
- Math skills

According to the job description, the right job candidate should have the ability to work independently. That very much fits with the way I do my best work, too.

根據職位描述，求職者應該具有獨立工作的能力。這工作方式非常適合我。

範例

參考回答範例（一）

1-5.3-05

According to the job description, the right job candidate should have the ability to work in a team. That very much fits with the way I do my best work, too. I really enjoy working in a team environment, and I get along well with colleagues. In my past work experience, I implemented a system to help organize the communication between colleagues so as to enhance our productivity as a team. It **indeed** （的確） helped us delegate tasks more easily, which led to earlier completion dates.

根據職位描述，求職者應該具有團隊合作的能力。這工作方式非常適合我。我非常喜歡在團隊環境中工作，與同事相處融洽。在我過去的工作經驗中，我曾引進一個系統幫助促進同事之間的交流，從而提高團隊的生產力。的而且確，該系統使我們能更輕鬆地分工，從而提前完成日期。

參考回答範例（二）

1-5.3-06

Though I enjoy working alone, I am also a great team player. Working with colleagues has taught me how to avoid **conflicts**（衝突）and make **compromises**（妥協）. In general, I think my team playing ability is in balance with my individual performance.

儘管我比較喜歡一個人工作，但也有很高的團隊精神。與同事一起工作教會了我如何避免衝突和達成妥協。總的來說，我覺得我的團隊合作能力和獨立工作表現一樣。

參考回答範例（三）

1-5.3-07

I have worked on teams and independently as well. Some tasks require a teamwork effort, while others fit individual work. In my previous job, I was mainly responsible for providing technical support. In addition to working individually, I have had opportunities to work in a team on **an impromptu basis**（無準備的，即興的）as well. I have immensely **enjoyed**（非常享受）playing both roles, and I think that I would be comfortable in both roles, that of a team member as well as a sole entity.

我既與別人合作過也單獨工作過。有的任務適合團隊合作，而另一些則適合單獨工作。在上一份工作中，我主要負責提供技術支援。除了單獨工作之外，我也有機會與他人暫時性地進行團隊合作。我非常享受同時扮演兩個角色──作為一個團隊成員和獨立個體。我覺得兩個角色對我而言都相當輕鬆。

小貼士

切忌讓對方感到你只能獨自工作，無法與人合作，或只能與人合作，無法獨自工作。雖然有偏好實屬正常，然而，很多公司也希望員工既能夠獨立工作，也能和團隊合作。所以，千萬不要暗示或明示自己只能取其一。換而言之，假如你確實喜歡在小組中工作，請明確說明你也能夠獨立工作的。相反，如果你喜歡獨立工作，請告訴面試官你也會考慮其他人的意見。

錯誤示範

I love working in a team because working alone is really boring.
我喜歡在團隊中工作，因為一個人工作真的很無聊。

📌 I don't like working alone, and I hate silence.

我不喜歡一個人工作，因為我討厭寧靜。

📌 I don't like working in a team because I work better and faster alone.

我不喜歡在團隊中工作，因為我獨自工作比較好和有效率。

📌 I don't like working in a team because I like to be the only responsible of my success.

我不喜歡在團隊中工作，因為我喜歡獨自為成功負責。

Question 2

Can you work under high pressure?

你可以在高壓下工作嗎？

1-5.3-08

其他類似問法

How do you work under pressure?

你在壓力下如何工作？

在求職面試中，其中一道頗常見的問題就是「你是否能在壓力下工作」，目的是了解面試者在職場上「實戰」的能力。在現今的社會，工作崗位上，很多時候我們都需要面對排山倒海的工作，可是工作時間卻總是相當有限的。所以我們總是要以「最少的時間」完成「最多的工作」，久而久之，壓力也隨之而生。「能否在壓力下工作」亦因此而成為職場上一項不可缺少的技能。

有些公司很在意員工是否適應在壓力下工作，原因很簡單，這是因為一間公司裏面的每一個員工都好比一台機器裏的一顆齒輪，只要有任何一顆「齒輪」在操作上出現問題，整台「機器」都會因此而無法正常的運作。所以，不少公司為着公司得以順利的運作，都希望能夠聘請一些能在壓力下工作、有能力在有限時間內完成工作的員工。

面試官問「你是否能在壓力下工作」這問題的話，其實主要是想知道：

- 你的抗壓能力如何；
- 你能否能夠在節奏急速且高要求的環境下高效地完成工作；
- 你是否已經準備好了用 200% 的能量去完成工作；
- 你的決斷能力、應變能力 、組織能力與掌控能力如何。

在這時候，你需要讓面試官知道你是一個恪守本分、臨危不亂的人，而且要極力讓對方相信你是一個能在危急關頭冷靜分析大局，並且於壓力下高效完成工作的員工。

Useful words & expressions

concurrently (adv.)	同時地
to prioritize my responsibilities (v phr.)	排列好優先等級
to put in extra effort (v phr.)	付出額外的努力
to create a detailed schedule (v phr.)	制定詳細的時間表
to organize my work into small assignments (v phr.)	對任務進行細化，把它們分組成一個一個的小任務
to reduce my own stress (v phr.)	減輕自己的壓力
strict deadline(s) (n phr.)	嚴格的期限
to maintain accuracy (v phr.)	保持準確性
limited resource(s) (n phr.)	更好地專注於手頭上的任務

■ 必學句型

🖈 I was used to _____ (e.g. meeting strict deadlines).

我習慣了 _____（+NP/G）。

🖈 In my previous role as _____, I always had to _____.

以前當我擔任 _____ 時，我經常需要 _____。

🖈 Thanks to this invaluable experience, _____.

多得這種寶貴的經驗，_____。

🖈 Frankly speaking, I _____.

坦白說，我 _____。

🖈 The solution is _____.

解決方法是 _____。

🖈 I will _____ (e.g. focus on the task) rather than _____(e.g. feeling panic 恐慌).

我會 _____ 而不是 _____（+NP/G）。

■ 簡短回答

🖈 I will focus on the task at hand rather than feeling stressed.

我會專注於當前的任務而非其壓力。

🖈 The solution is not to panic but to remain focused on delivering my very best.

秘訣是不要驚慌，然後保持專注、盡我所能。

📌 This enables me to channel my energy into accomplishing tasks efficiently.

這能使我將精力投放到任務中並能高效完成，從而轉化成收穫。

📌 I believe I deal with pressure well.

我相信我能順利應對壓力。

參考回答範例（一）

1-5.3-12

Frankly speaking（坦白說）, I am able to thrive under **multiple**（多個）deadlines and projects. For example, in my previous job, I once had to work on six projects which were all due in the same month. However, by **prioritizing** my responsibilities（把……排列好優先等級）, working effectively with my team members and putting in **extra effort**（付出額外的努力）, I was able to complete all these projects ahead of time effectively.

坦白說，壓力能使我進步。例如，在上一份工作中，曾經有一次我需要在一個月內完成六個大型項目。在排列好六個項目的優先等級後，我和團隊成員合力付出額外的努力完成工作。結果，我們在期限內提前完成了工作。

參考回答範例（二）

1-5.3-13

In my previous role as a **customer service assistant**（客戶服務助理）, I always had to work under pressure. **Thanks to**（得益於／基於／多得）this invaluable experience, I feel I have become a better worker who is able to handle a number of tasks **concurrently**（同時地）. When I had to deal with several unsatisfied customers, I would focus on the task at hand rather than feeling stressed. I believe that my ability to communicate effectively with customers helps reduce my own stress as well as any stress the customer may feel.

以前當我擔任客戶服務助理時，壓力無處不在。但也正正因為這些寶貴的經驗，我學會了同時處理多項任務，也使我成為了一名更好的員工。每當我需要同時處理一些比較棘手的顧客時，我都會專注於當前的任務而非其壓力。我相信與客戶溝通的能力有助於減輕我自己的壓力以及安撫客戶，問題也變得更加容易處理。

參考回答範例（三）

1-5.3-14

When I was a university student, I was used to coping with high-pressure assignments and meeting strict deadlines whilst maintaining accuracy. At the same time, I had to deal with various society events with limited resources. Honestly speaking, I've found that I enjoy working in a challenging environment and I'm able to produce some of my best work when under pressure.

當我還是一名大學生時，我已經習慣了在壓力下工作，包括在限期前完成作業同時確保其準確性。此外，我亦需要利用有限的資源來處理各式各樣的學會活動。老實說，我發現我挺喜歡在充滿挑戰的環境底下工作，並且在壓力下，我也能把工作做到最好。

小貼士

1 切忌說你從來沒有壓力

每個人在工作中或多或少都會有一定的壓力,這是很正常的。所以當面試官問你'Can you work under high pressure?'時,千萬不要說你從來沒有壓力,否則會使對方認為你為人不夠誠實和勤勉的。

錯誤示範

To be honest, I never feel stressed.
說實話,我從不感到有壓力。

2 切忌把重點放在面對壓力時的感受

這是一場面試而非心理諮詢。面試官不會太在意你於面對壓力時的心理感受,你對待壓力的方式和緩解壓力的能力才是他們關注的地方。

錯誤示範

Although deadlines make me nervous and stressed, I will try to manage my time well in order to get things done.
儘管截止期限會使我感到緊張和有壓力,但我會盡力安排自己的時間以完成任務。

3 切忌說自己有時會被壓力打敗

記住,你要把回答的重點放在「如何應對壓力」,讓面試官相信你是一個具有應對壓力能力的人。

錯誤示範

To be frank, sometimes I get beaten by pressure.
坦白說,我有時會被壓力打敗。

求職相關的問題

Question 1

What is your greatest weakness?
你最大的弱點是甚麼？

1-5.4-01

其他類似問法

What do you think is your biggest weakness?

你認為你最大的弱點是甚麼？

What are your weaknesses?

你的弱點是甚麼？

前《哈佛商業評論》總編輯蘇西・韋爾奇（Suzy Welch）曾說過，面試官詢問求職者這問題一般是為了了解他的性格特點、思維方式、知識能力，從而衡量對方能否勝任自己所應徵的職位。Suzy Welch 亦表示，如果想要把問題回答得漂亮，首要的要素就是「誠實」。因此，對待這個問題，我們只好真誠地暴露自己的弱點，並主動提供針對這弱點的解決方案。

值得留意的是，這個「弱點」千萬不能是應徵職位的「致命傷」。如果你去應聘會計，你能否跟面試官說自己比較粗心大意？應聘銷售，能否跟面試官說自己比較內向害羞？如果你真的這樣回答了，面試官會留下這樣的印象：「這個人很老實，但不適合這崗位。」

記住，面試官真正想知道的事情，是你到底清不清楚自己的能力，還有你有否為自己的不足積極計劃改進方案，及是否正為此作出努力。以下，筆者為大家準備了必學詞彙、短語，以及回答範例，教你如何讓面試官眼睛一亮，進而在面試中脫穎而出。

List of weaknesses

- Insecure (adj.)
  缺乏安全感的

1-5.4-02

- Extremely Introverted (adj.)
  極度內向的

- Extremely Extroverted (adj.)
  極度外向

- Too detail-oriented (adj.)
  過於注重細節

- Too sensitive (adj.)
  太敏感

求職相關的問題

- Too straight-forward (adj.)
  太直率

- Have trouble saying 'no' (v phr.)
  不太懂說「不」

- Have trouble asking for help (v phr.)
  不太懂尋求別人幫助

- Lack confidence (v phr.)
  缺乏信心

回答「缺點是甚麼」的步驟如下：

第一步	• 真誠地暴露自己的弱點
第二步	• 主動提供針對這弱點的解決方案 / 展示自己正為此弱點作出最大努力去改善

1-5.4-03

第一步：真誠地暴露自己的弱點

Useful words & expressions

Anxious (adj.)	焦慮的
Patience (n.)	耐心
Patient (adj.)	有耐性的
Self-sufficient (adj.)	自給自足
To rely on somebody (v phr.)	依靠某人
To work independently (v phr.)	獨立工作
A sign of weakness (n phr.)	軟弱的表現
Lead to (v phr.)	導致
Result in (v phr.)	造成
Frustrated (adj.)	沮喪的
Timid (adj.)	膽小的
To provide constructive feedback (v phr.)	提供建設性的意見
To be frank (v phr.)	坦白説
Nervous (adj.)	緊張的

When I'm too excited or anxious, I may talk very fast.

當我太興奮或焦慮時，我可能會把話說得很快。

When working with colleagues, I may not have much patience as I am quite self-sufficient. So, it's somehow a bit difficult when I have to rely on others to complete my work. That's the reason why I've pursued roles that require someone to work independently.

與同事一起工作時，我可能沒有足夠的耐心，因為我習慣自己滿足自己的需求。因此，當我不得不依靠他人來完成工作時，這某種程度上有點困難，這是為甚麼我一直尋找需要獨立工作的職位。

I have a hard time sharing a task with others because I always tell me myself that I can do it all on my own. In the past, I misunderstood that asking for help was a sign of weakness. This has led to me taking on projects that have overwhelmed me and resulted in me being frustrated and angry.

過去的我很難與他人一起做任務，因為我總是告訴自己可以獨自完成所有事情。以往的我誤解了尋求幫助是一種軟弱的表現，導致因面對過量的工作而沮喪和憤怒。

Sometimes, I may be timid when providing constructive feedback to colleagues, out of fear of hurting someone's feelings.

有時，當需要向同事提供建設性的意見時，我可能會因擔心傷害別人的感受而卻步。

📌 To be frank, public speaking makes me nervous.
坦白說，公開演講讓我感到緊張。

第二步：提供針對這弱點的解決方案 /
展示自己正改善這弱點

1-5.4-05

Useful words & expressions

To overcome this problem, I_____ (phr.)	為了克服這個問題，我 _____
To remind myself to____(v phr.)	提醒自己 _____
To take a deep breath (v phr.)	深呼吸
Occasionally (adv.)	偶爾
I've learned to recognize that_____ (phr.)	我學會了 _____
Work standards (n phr.)	工作標準
To respect (v.)	尊重
Working style (n phr.)	工作作風
To enrol in _____ (v phr.)	報名參加 _____
Workshop (n.)	工作坊
To ask for outside help (v phr.)	向外部尋求協助
I realized (that) _____(phr.)	我意識到 _____
Since then (phr.)	從那時起；自此之後
I'm actively working on _____ (phr.)	我正在積極致力於 _____

簡短回答

📌 To overcome this, I remind myself to take a deep breath, address my pace, and slow down. I've learned to replenish my breath by pausing occasionally, every 6 to 8 words.

為了克服這個問題,我提醒自己要深呼吸、注意自己的節奏,然後放慢節奏。我也學會了每說 6 到 8 個字就稍微停一停,以補充呼吸。

📌 I'm actively working on making sure that my criticisms are constructive.

我正在積極努力,以確保我的批評具有建設性。

📌 I've worked hard to improve this weakness by, for example, enrolling in team building workshops. While I typically work independently, it's also important for me to learn how to trust my co-workers and ask for outside help when necessary.

然而,我一直以來也在努力改善這種弱點,例如參加團隊建設工作坊。儘管我習慣獨立工作,但對我來說,學習如何信任同事並在必要時尋求他們的幫助也很重要的。

But now, I've learned to recognize that everyone has his or her work standards and levels of productivity. We should respect everyone's working style.

但是現在，我學會了認識到每個人都有他的工作標準和效率。我們應該尊重每個人的工作作風。

In my previous role, sometimes I had to edit my team member's work and provide feedback for areas of improvement. Through this experience, I realized that feedback can be both helpful and kind, when delivered the right way. Since then, I've become better at offering feedback, and I've realized that my empathy can be used to my advantage to provide thoughtful and productive feedback.

在上一份工作，我間中也需編輯團隊成員的工作成果，並提供意見以供改進。這經驗不但讓我獲益良多，同時意識到以正確的方式給予他人意見的好處 —— 既可表示友好，亦能達到相得益彰之效。自此，我更樂於給予人意見，而這方面的能力亦隨之竿頭直上，與此同時，我亦意識到原來自己可運用同理心去為他人提供具建設性的意見，從而發揮優勢。

求職相關的問題

參考回答範例

1-5.4-07

When I was a tertiary student, I was used to coping with high-pressure assignments and meeting strict deadlines. Therefore, I'm used to working at high pace.

當我還是一名大專生時，我習慣了應付高壓的作業和嚴格地看待截止日期。因此，我習慣了高效工作。

〔真誠地暴露自己的弱點〕：Sometimes when my colleagues perform tasks at a slower pace than I do, I may feel frustrated.

有時當我的同事以比我慢的速度執行任務時，我可能會感到沮喪。

〔展示自己正為此弱點作出最大努力去改善〕：But now, I've learned to recognize that everyone has his or her work standards and levels of productivity. We should respect everyone's working style. In my previous job, I was responsible for ensuring all the deadlines were met. In order not to interrupt my co-workers progress with a visit or a call, I used Smartsheet, a work-execution tool to track tasks and due dates. For example, I set alerts, updates, and reminders for them.

但是現在我學會了認識到每個人都有他的工作標準和效率，我們應該尊重每個人的工作作風。在上一份工作中，我負責確保工作都在限期內完成。為了不打斷同事的工作，我使用了工作表執行工具 Smartsheet 來觀察任務的進度和到期日。例如，我為它們設置了預報、更新和提醒。

小貼士

切忌說自己沒有缺點，導致顯得自己過份虛偽和自大。

錯誤示範

My weakness? I don't think I have any big weaknesses. If you really need me to think of one weakness, I guess you could say I work too hard. In fact, that's because I care too much about every job I'm doing. Yea...I'm a perfectionist. Everytime when I'm handling a task, I have to make sure it's absolutely 100% right.

我的弱點？我認為我沒有甚麼太大的缺點。如果您真的需要我說出一個弱點，或許您可以說我工作太努力了。實際上，那是因為我太在意所做的每一項工作。我是一名完美主義者。每次處理任務時，我都必須確保它絕對是 100％正確的。

Can you tell me what your greatest strength is?

你能告訴我你最大的優點是甚麼？

1-5.4-08

其他類似問法

What do you think is your greatest strength?

你認為你最大的優點是甚麼？

What are your strengths?

你的優點是甚麼？

---

* 其實在這個問題上，面試官關注的問題有兩點：

• 求職者是否坦誠、是否真的能證明自己的優勢。

• 求職者所具備的優點是不是這個職位所需要的特質。

要得到這份工作，你必須要體現出自己的獨特性、不可替代性。嘗試挑選出令人印象深刻的經歷，自信地向面試官展現自己的優勢。記住，你所提及的的優勢要與職位需求一致。在準備面試時，你需要仔細研究招聘廣告中的職位描述和職責。

回答時，可以描述過往的實習或工作中與應聘職位所需要的能力相關的經歷，用詳細例子作支撐來證明自己的優勢。

以下，筆者為大家準備了必學詞彙、短語，以及回答範例，教你如何讓面試官眼睛一亮，進而在面試中脫穎而出。

List of Strengths

1-5.4-09

- Creative (adj.) 有創意的

- Flexible (adj.) 靈活

- Be good at taking Initiative (v phr.) 善於採取主動行動

- Honest (adj.) 誠實的

- Continuous Learning (n phr.) 持續學習

- Self-control (n.) 自制的；自控的

- Action-oriented (adj.) 行動派的

- Entrepreneurial (adj.) 企業家的

- Attentive (adj.) 留心的

- Detail-oriented (adj.) 注意細節的

- Collaborative (adj.) 合作的

- Disciplined (adj.) 有紀律的

- Empathetic (adj.) 善解人意的

- Enthusiastic (adj.) 熱心的

- Versatile (adj.) 多功能的

- Innovative (adj.) 有創意的；創新的

- Patient (adj.) 有耐心的

Useful words & expressions

Strong organization skills (n phr.)	較強的組織能力
To think out-of-the-box (v phr.)	跳出框框；開拓思路
Be good at thinking strategically (v phr.)	善於策略性思考
Varied (adj.)	多種多樣的；多變的
I pride myself on _____ (phr.)	我以自己能 ____ 感到驕傲
Flexible (adj.)	靈活的；有彈性的
Reliable (adj.)	可靠的
A "get it done" mentality (n phr.)	一種「做得到的」的心態
Methodical (adj.)	有條不紊的
Conscientious (adj.)	認真負責的
Reputation (n.)	聲譽
To meet deadlines (v phr.)	在限期前完成工作
Strategically (adv.)	有策略地；戰略性地
To keep track of... (v phr.)	為了跟進……

■ 必學句型

📌 I have strong_____skills.
我有很強的 _____ 技能。

1-5.4-11

📌 I'm good at _____.
我擅長 _____。

📌 I'm passionate about_____.
我對 _____ 充滿熱情。

📌 My real strength is_____.
我的真正強項是 _____。

📌 I believe that my biggest strength lies in my ability to_____.
我相信我最大的優勢在於我的 _____ 能力。

■ 簡短回答

📌 I have strong organization skills and am good at strategically thinking through business issues to help grow the company.
我有很強的組織能力，並且擅長從商業角度進行戰略思考，以幫助公司發展。

1-5.4-12

📌 I've always preferred to collaborate with people and find that my collaborative nature is one of my strongest attributes.
我一直以來也喜歡與人合作，並且發現我的合作天性是我最強的特質之一。

求職相關的問題

📌 I'm good at thinking out-of-the-box, curious about new things, extremely passionate about machine learning and its applications.

我擅長於跳出框框、對新事物感到好奇、對機器學習及其應用充滿熱情。

📌 My real strength is my attention to detail. I'm a methodical and conscientious person, and I pride myself on my reputation for "meeting deadlines". When I commit to doing something, I make sure it gets done on time.

我是一個有條不紊、認真負責的人，我為自己擁有「能在截止日期前完成工作」的良好聲譽而感到自豪。當我承諾做某事時，我確保它按時完成。

📌 I believe that my biggest strength lies in my ability to adapt to changing situations. When something unexpected happens, I readily change gears in response. I am aware that the role of a secretary is a varied one and I pride myself on being flexible and reliable with a "get-it-done" mentality.

我相信我最大的優勢在於能夠適應不斷變化的情況。當發生意外情況時，我能隨時換檔。我知道秘書的職責是多種多樣的，我為自己以「做得到」的心態靈活的可靠而感到自豪。

範例

參考回答範例

1-5.4-13

I have strong organization skills and am good at strategically thinking through business issues to help grow the company.

我有很強的組織能力，並且擅長從商業角度進行戰略思考，以幫助公司發展。

（提供相關示例來豐富答案）：For example, a few months ago, my marketing manager wanted me to prepare some social media graphics for four different campaigns in the same month. I was responsible for delivering and posting around 8 to 10 graphics per week. To keep track of my progress, I made one main folder on Google Drive and created sub-folders for each campaign. I was able to meet all the deadlines that were set on a weekly basis.

例如，幾個月前，我的營銷經理要我在同一個月內為四個不同的廣告活動準備一些圖片用來上載至社交媒體。我負責每週分發和發佈大約 8 到 10 張圖。為了跟蹤工作進度，我在 Google 雲端硬盤上創建了一個主文件夾，並為每個廣告系列創建了子文件夾，確保我能在限期內完成工作。

Question 1

What are your career aspirations?
你的職業志向是甚麼？

1-5.5-01

> **其他類似問法**
>
> What is your career plan?
>
> **你有甚麼職業規劃？**
>
> What is your career plan for the next _____ years?
>
> **你對自己未來 _____ 年的職業規劃是甚麼？**

求職者在面試中會遇到各種各樣的提問。其中關於職業志向（Career Aspirations）的問題愈來愈受企業 HR 重視。職業志向通常是指長期的職業目標（a long-term career goal）、計劃或夢想，而不單單是短期的夢想。當面試官問你 "What are your career aspirations?" 時，其實對方是希望了解你對這份工作的態度，從而考察你自我規劃的能力，確定你的潛力是否符合他們公司的要求，進而方便日後為你制定職業生涯規劃。到底怎樣的回答才會受到 HR 的欣賞？

技巧

- 讓 HR 知道你是有備而來的。回答這問題時,要讓對方感覺到你是一個有計劃的、心思熟慮的求職者,而非漁翁撒網,胡亂投簡歷。

- 表明自己的優勢,讓對方感到你是這職位的不二人選。

- 面試前,必須經過一番冷靜思考,並為自己樹立一個明確的目標,繼而清楚地規劃未來 3 至 5 年的計劃和打算,務求在被問到自己的 career aspirations 時,能表明你是符合應聘公司要求的穩定型員工。

- 例:謹慎的想清楚若干年後,自己到底想在公司晉升到一個甚麼位置。

1-5.5-02

Useful words & expressions

to aspire to (v. phr.)	渴望
timeframe (n.)	時間表;大概時間
to mentor (v phr.)	指導
professional(s) (n.)	專業人士
definitely (adv.)	確實地;肯定底;無疑地

enterprise businesses (n phr.)	企業業務
product development (n phr.)	產品開發
sought-after (adj.)	熱門的;被追捧的;高度青睞的
in high demand (prep phr.)	需求量大
strategically (adv.)	戰略性地
skillfully (adv.)	熟練地
to be exposed to sth (v phr.)	接觸
to gain insight into sth (n phr.)	深入了解某事
tactical career goal(s) (n phr.)	策略性的職業目標
long-term (adj.)	長期的;長遠的
short-term (adj.)	短期的
ideally (adj.)	最理想的是;理想地
a broad set of skills (n phr.)	廣泛的技能
ins and outs (n phr.)	來龍去脈

1-5.5-03

When I think of my career aspirations, I think of a timeframe maybe _____ years from now.

當論及自己的職業志向時，我想到的大概是 _____ 的日子。

I aspire to have the ability to _____.

我渴望有能力 _____。

I definitely aspire to be exposed to _____ (+NP/G).

我非常渴望接觸 _____。

I hope to move into a position as a/an _____ within ___ years.

我希望在 ___ 年內升任 _____ 一職。

I aspire to be able to gain insight into _____.

我渴望能夠深入了解 _____。

I aspire to obtain _____.

我渴望能夠獲得 _____。

I would like to be trained as a/an _____ so that I can benefit you further.

我想接受 _____ 的培訓，以便我進一步為您公司帶來收益。

My biggest career goal is to _____.

我最大的職業目標是 _____。

I aspire to grow into a/an _____ position and _____.

我渴望能晉升為 _____，並 _____。

簡短回答

1-5.5-04

When I think of my career aspirations, I think of a timeframe maybe 5 to 8 years from now.

當論及自己的職業志向時，我想到的大概是未來 5 至 8 年的日子。

I aspire to have the ability to manage and mentor my own team of marketing professionals.

我渴望有能力管理和指導自己的營銷專家團隊。

I definitely aspire to be exposed to managing a team.

我非常渴望接觸管理團隊。

I hope to move into a position as a production manager in 8 years.

我希望在 8 年內升任生產經理。

I aspire to be able to gain insight into the healthcare system and bridge communication between healthcare providers and patients.

我渴望能夠深入了解醫療保健系統，並架起醫療保健提供者與患者之間的溝通橋樑。

I aspire to obtain a stronger track record of result making.

我渴望能夠獲得更佳的業績記錄。

I would like to be trained as a software designer so that, over time, I can benefit you further.

我想接受軟件設計師的培訓，以便進一步為您公司帶來收益。

📌 I aspire to grow into a leadership position and teach newcomers the ins and outs of retail sales.

我渴望能晉升為領導者，並負責教導新入行的員工有關零售業的來龍去脈。

範例

參考回答範例（一）

1-5.5-05

To be frank, I have some pretty lofty career aspirations. After researching your company and learning more about this position, I feel that this role fits well with my future aspirations. I'd love to see myself promoted based on my hard work and results, eventually managing one of the branches, then become a regional director.

坦白說，我的確有一些頗崇高的職業抱負。在研究您的公司並更深入了解這個職位後，我覺得這個職位很適合我的未來抱負。我很希望能靠自己辛勤的工作和成果而升職，最終能負責管理其中一個分行，繼而成為區域總監。

範例

參考回答範例（二）

1-5.5-06

When I think of my career aspirations, I think of a timeframe maybe 5 years from now. So far, my biggest career goal is to handle multi-million dollar campaigns and accounts. As far as I know, your company has a number of critical clients who are taken care of by only your top marketers. My career goal in the coming 5 years is to become part of that marketing team.

當我想到自己的職業理想時，我想大約 5 年後可以實踐。到目前為止，我最大的職業目標是處理數百萬元的活動和客戶。據我所知， 貴公司有許多僅由您的頂級營銷人員照顧的重要客戶。我在未來 5 年的職業目標是成為該營銷團隊的一員。

參考回答範例（三）

1-5.5-07

I have a **passion**（熱情）for human resources. I **long for**（渴望）new challenges and wish to embrace a different environment where I can better express my **capabilities**（能力）. Particularly, I enjoy working with employees to improve their quality of life through support and communication. One of my main career goals is to develop my knowledge of **human capital management**（人力資本管理）and promote **a variety of**（各項）employee wellness programs. Within the next 8 years, I aspire to move into a position as a **Human Resources Director**（人力資源總監）so that I can facilitate professional development, training, and activities for HR staff. Besides, I definitely hope to plan, lead, **coordinate**（協調）, and **implement**（實施）training programs.

我對人力資源充滿熱情。我渴望新的挑戰，並希望在一個可以更好地表現自己能力的環境中工作。我特別喜歡與員工合作，並通過支持和溝通來改善他們的生活質素。我的主要職業目標之一是發展我對人力資本管理的知識，並促進各項員工健康計劃。在接下來的 8 年中，我渴望擔任人力資源總監一職，以便為人力資源人員提供專業發展、培訓和活動。此外，我非常希望可以計劃、領導、協調和實施公司的培訓計劃。

求職相關的問題

Question 1

Why is there a gap in your work history?

為甚麼你的工作經歷中出現了「空窗期」？

1-5.6-01

其他類似問法

Why didn't you get a job until now?

為甚麼直到現在你都沒有找到工作？

Why have you been jobless for three months?

你為甚麼失業了 3 個月？

Why have you been unemployed for such a long time?

你為甚麼失業這麼長時間？

Where was there an employment gap on your resume?

為甚麼你的履歷表中出現了「工作空窗期」？

要記住，幾個月的「空窗期」或許沒關係，但是如果你的「空窗期」長達數年，就要好好計劃一下如何回答，才能讓對方有信心聘請你了。職業空窗期本不是甚麼反常的事，你愈是想隱瞞就愈是惹人注意。僱主想要的是你對工作的熱情以及重入職場的準備，只要你能表現這些重點，並且解釋為何你認為你適合這個職位，必能重回職場。

不少人因為各種原因而出現「工作空窗期」，而當你再去找新的工作的時候，你應該如何說明呢？其實，無論你是出於甚麼理由都務必清晰明確的告知面試官，現在的你已經收拾好心情，可隨時全力投入工作，並且擁有「非常正面的工作態度」，讓他不用擔心你隨時又有需要放大假或辭職。

常見的「工作空窗期」原因

- Caring for a family member 照顧家庭成員

- Health issue 健康問題

- Pursuing further education 繼續進修

1-5.6-02

- Taking time off to travel, study, work on a solo project, etc.
  騰出時間去旅行、學習，或專注個人項目等

- Trying to start a business 嘗試創業

- Trying to start a freelance career 嘗試從事自由職業

- Spending time finding a job after being laid off
  被解僱後需要花時間找工作

如果是因為出去旅遊或者靜心修養了一段日子，可以實話實說。你可以說一下自己在旅遊的過程中見識了甚麼、感悟了甚麼；或是修養期間看了甚麼書，令你對人生的規劃有了不一樣的想法（一定是要和應聘的職位有關連的事物）。

如果是創業的話，你可以告訴對方自己當初創業的思想，以及失敗的原因，並總結一下箇中的得着（當然是與應聘的職位有關連的），說不定還能引起對方的共鳴。

如果是因為健康原因，或者需要照顧家人，如長者及小朋友，則平常敘述帶過即可。最緊要表現出你的行動力和堅強就可以了。記住記住記住！千萬不要煽情博取同情，否則只會帶來反效果。

預備好充分的理由後，可遵循以下的步驟解釋自己的「工作空窗期」：

第一步	• 清楚、簡短地向面試官說明該情況。 • 不需要描述過多的個人訊息，只需告訴對方核心內容（the core facts）便可。
第二步	• 說明上述情況已經結束或者對你來說已經不再是一個問題，讓僱主知道他不必擔心你再次需要另一個「工作空窗期」。最緊要告知面試官自己已經 100% 準備好投入該職位。
第三步	• 重申自己對該職位深感興趣，並將重點放在此面試和職位上。

範例

根據上述三部曲的應對範例

1-5.6-03

第一步：清楚、簡短地向面試官說明該情況

"I took about a year off last year to care for my grandmother during an illness. I spent some time as the primary caretaker for her"…

（我去年休假了大約一年，以照顧我生病的祖母。我亦成為了她主要的看護人一段日子。）

第二步：說明上述情況已經結束或者對你來說已經不再是一個問題

…"Now my grandmother is under full-time care, and I am ready and eager to get back to full-time work."…

（現在，我的祖母有了專人全職照顧，而我也準備好並渴望回到全職工作。）

第三步：重申自己對該職位深感興趣

…"Therefore, I've begun job searching and I'm focused on finding a data entry clerk position that will help me advance my career further now."

（因此，我開始尋找工作，並專注於尋找數據輸入員這職位，這將幫助我進一步發展自己的事業。）

The primary caretaker (n phr.)	主要看護人
New-born baby (n phr.)	初生嬰兒
Health issue (n phr.)	健康問題
Further education (n phr.)	進修;持續教育
Start-up company (n phr.)	初創公司
Freelancer (n.)	自由職業者
Be laid off (v phr.)	被解僱
Be eager to (v phr.)	渴望
To advance (v phr.)	推進
To undergo a restructuring(v phr.)	進行重組架構
To eliminate (v phr.)	消除 / 廢除
Haven't found the right fit (v phr.)	找不到合適的（工作）
To take on new challenges (v phr.)	迎接新挑戰
Injury (n.)	受傷

■ 必學句型

🔖 I had to quit my previous position to _____.
為了 _____，我不得不辭掉之前的工作。

🔖 In fact, I had always intended to go back to work once _____, and I am ready to do so now.
實際上，我一直打算等到 _____ 後就重新返回職場。

🔖 I am now seeking an opportunity to advance my career further and apply some of the _____ skills I gained while I was out of the workforce.
我現在已經準備好重新工作了，並正在尋找機會進一步發展自己的職業，且運用我在待業期間學到的一些 _____ 技巧。

🔖 My former employer underwent a restructuring and my position as a/an _____ had been eliminated.
我的前公司進行了重組，而我作為 _____ 的職位也被取消了。

🔖 I'm looking forward to the opportunity to apply those _____ experiences in my next job.
我期待着有機會在下一份工作中運用這些 _____ 經驗。

求職相關的問題

1-5.6-06

簡短回答

📌 I took about a year off last year after a shoulder injury.
去年，我因肩部受傷而休了一年假。

📌 I had to quit my previous position to care for my new-born baby.
為了照顧我的初生嬰兒，我不得不辭掉之前的工作。

📌 In fact, I had always intended to go back to work once my child was in school, and I am ready to do so now.
實際上，我一直打算等到孩子上學後就重新返回職場。

📌 I am now seeking an opportunity to advance my career further and apply some of the writing skills I gained while I was out of the workforce.
我現在已經準備好重新工作了，並正在尋找機會進一步發展自己的職業，且運用我在待業期間學到的一些寫作技巧。

📌 My former employer underwent a restructuring and my position as a receptionist had been eliminated.
我的前公司進行了重組，而我接待員的職位也被取消了。

📌 I'm looking forward to the opportunity to apply those marketing experiences in my next job.
我期待着在下一份工作中運用這些營銷經驗。

求職英語一本通

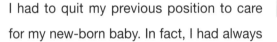

範例

參考回答範例（一）

1-5.6-07

I had to quit my previous position to care for my new-born baby. In fact, I had always intended to go back to work once he was in school, and I am ready to do so now. I am now seeking an opportunity to advance my career further and apply some of the writing skills I gained while I was out of the workforce, including some online language courses I took in the evening.

為了照顧我的初生嬰兒，我不得不辭掉之前的工作。實際上，我一直打算等到他上學後就重新返回職場。我現在已經準備好重新工作了，並正在尋找機會進一步發展自己的事業，且運用我在待業期間學到的一些寫作技巧，當中包括一些晚間線上語言課程所學到的技巧。

範例

參考回答範例（二）

1-5.6-08

My former employer underwent a restructuring and my position as a data entry clerk had been eliminated. Frankly speaking, it was a difficult time, but I left with the confidence that I had developed important skills there and built strong relationships with my managers and colleagues. I'm looking forward to the opportunity to apply those experiences in my next job.

我的前公司重組架構，而我數據輸入文員的職位也被取消了。坦白說，那是一個艱難的時期，但我還是滿懷信心地離開了那裏。我在前公司學到重要的技能，並與我的經理和同事建立了牢固的關係。現在，我正期待着在下一份工作中運用這些經驗。

Question 2

What is your expected salary?
你期望的薪資是多少？

1-5.6-09

其他類似問法

What are your salary expectations?

你的預期薪資是多少？

What do you expect in the way of salary?

你對薪資的期望如何？

What salary range would you require to take this job?

你期望這份工作的薪資範圍是多少？

職場中，找工作必須得先通過面試官的考核，當面試進行到尾聲時，HR 總會問求職者："What is your expected salary?" 這個時候，求職者到底要如何回答才不會自貶身價，又不會令對方覺得你「叫價太高」而將你拒之門外？大多數公司的在招聘廣告都不會把工資明確列明，所以最好的辦法是不直接正面回答，給自己留一定餘地。

想要有技巧地應對這問題，關鍵是根據自己能力與職位的匹配程度作答。

小貼士

回答時應注意以下兩點：

1 了解行情

一般來說，同一行業中的公司經營管理模式其實都大同小異，所以相同或者相似的職位的薪金理論上也都不會差太多。在面試前最好事先了解目標職能在行業內的薪資範圍（例如：底線是多少？頂薪又能達到多少？）這些都是期望薪資的重要參考數據。

2 認清自我，面試前衡量自己的價值

事實上，面試官詢問求職者的 expected salary 的另外一個原因是為了了解求職者對自我是否有足夠準確的認知。我們都知道面試官們閱人無數，其實他們在和求職者交談的過程中已經在內心給求職者定了一個理想的工資。若是求職者的 expected salary 和他內心定的價位差不多，說明這求職者認知不錯，也做了一定的功課。

假如求職者開價太進取，就會顯得激進好勝；開價太低的話，就會顯得為人謙虛或缺乏自信。因此，求職者面試前必須要做足功課，衡量一下自己能力與認證職位的匹配程度，這樣才能更準確判斷自己的價值，從而提出讓對方滿意的期望工資。

有專家建議，在回答有關薪金的問題時，可以有技巧地拖延回答，避免立即給予對方一個實質的數字。因此，在回答有關薪金的問題時，你可以先說：

✓ I'm actually more interested in finding a position that's a good fit for my skills and interests. I believe that you will be offering a salary that's competitive in the current market.
實際上，我對找到一個適合我的技能和興趣的職位更感興趣。我相信您將提供一個在當前市場上合理的薪金。
(＊簡單來說，你要巧妙地讓面試官知道你對自己的能力充滿信心。同時，你希望對方能提供一個合理的工資以表示對你的尊重。)

當然，若面試官發現你沒有直接透露自己的期望工資，有可能會再次詢問一次，務求令你直接回應問題。這時候，你可以說：

✓ Well, based on my research and past experience, my understanding is that 22K to 25K per month is typical for this role.
好吧，根據我的研究和過去的經驗，我的理解是，這個職位一般有 $22,000 到 $25,000 月薪。

1-5.6-10

Useful words & expressions

Mutually (adv.)	雙互；雙方
Starting salary (n phr.)	起薪點
Range (n.)	範圍
Be open to negotiation (v phr.)	願意談判
Remuneration (n.)	報酬；薪金
Skillsets (n.)	技能
Align with _____ (v phr.)	與 _____ 一致
To further discuss (v phr.)	進一步討論
Budget (n.)	預算
Commission structure (n phr.)	佣金結構

求職相關的問題

■ 必學句型

🖈 Before discussing money, I'd like to know more about the _____ position and its duties first. But may I ask what salary range you're considering for this position?

在討論金錢之前,我想先了解更多有關 _____ 的職位及其職責。但是,請問您考慮提供的薪水範圍是多少?

🖈 Before we get into the remuneration, I'd like to discuss more about the expectations of the _____ position. If my skillsets align with what the job requires of me, we can proceed to further discuss about my starting salary.

在討論報酬之前,我想討論更多關於 _____ 一職的期望。如果我的技能與工作要求一致的話,我們可以繼續討論我的起薪。

🖈 From the research that I have done, it appears to be in the $_____ to $_____ range. Is that the range you had in mind?

根據我所做的研究,工資水平似乎在 _____ 至 _____ 之間。請問那是您所定的範圍嗎?

With regard to my expected salary, I am looking for around $_____ per month. Nevertheless, I am open to negotiation and discussing with you till we come to a mutually agreeable starting salary.

關於我的期望薪金，我期望能得到大約 _____ 月薪。不過，在我們達成雙方同意的起薪之前，我願意與您進行談判和討論。

■ 簡短回答

1-5.6-12

Before we get into the remuneration, I'd like to discuss more about the expectations of the sales representation position. If my skillsets align with what the job requires of me, we can proceed to further discuss about my starting salary.

在討論報酬之前，我想討論更多關於銷售代表一職的期望。如果我的技能與工作要求一致的話，我們可以繼續討論我的起薪。

With regard to my expected salary, I am looking for around $17,000 per month. Nevertheless, I am open to negotiation and discussing with you till we come to a mutually agreeable starting salary.

關於我的期望薪金，我期望能得到月薪 $17,000。不過，在我們達成雙方同意的起薪之前，我願意與您進行談判和討論。

I think I need more information about this position before we start to discuss salary. May I postpone that discussion until later? It would be great if you could tell me what is budgeted for the position, and how your commission structure works.

我認為在開始討論薪資之前，我需要了解更多有關這職位的資料。我們可以之後再討論這話題嗎？倘若您能告訴我該職位的預算是多少，以及其佣金結構如何運作，那就太好了。

I'm sure that when the time comes and I know more about this role, we can come to a mutually agreeable figure.

我相信當時機到了，加上我對這個職位有了更多的了解時，我們可以達成一個雙方同意的數字。

From the research that I have done, it appears to be in the $18,000 to $22,000 range. Is that the range you had in mind?

根據我所做的研究，工資水平似乎在 18,000 元至 22,000 元之間。請問那是您所定的範圍嗎？

Before discussing money, I'd like to know more about the software engineer position and its duties first. But may I ask what salary range you're considering for this position?

在討論金錢之前，我想先了解更多有關軟件工程師的職位及其職責。但是，請問您考慮提供的薪水範圍是多少？

Chapter

06 如何向
主考官提問

一般而言，在面試時，面試官會問你一系列有關「應聘這份工作的原因」、「個人特質」、「職業志向」等等的問題。而在面試接近尾聲時，面試官總是喜歡詢問求職者有沒有任何問題想提出 (e.g. "Is there anything else you would like to ask me?" 你有沒有甚麼想提問的？或 "Do you have any questions?" 你有甚麼問題想問嗎？)。

這時候，假如你回應 "No, thanks." 的話，那麼，你可能要有心理準備另覓一份工作了。其實，在很多主考官認定的「不錄取標準」中，其中一項就是「沒有提出與工作相關的問題」。倘若你真的對應聘的職位感興趣，定必有一些問題在腦海中，希望得到對方回答的。

因此在面試前，記得準備有關「應聘公司」、「應聘職位」、「工作內容」、「公司內部教育」以及「公司所面臨的情況」等問題，以利提問。

6.1 提出與工作相關的問題

到底在一場英文面試中要怎樣回答這個問題才能讓面試官眼前一亮呢？為了讓你能專業地應付面試的「最後一擊」，筆者已為你預備了一系列的問題。Let's go!

詢問「有關應聘公司的資訊」

1-6.1-01

🔖 Would your mind telling me how many employees you have in your company?

您能告訴我　貴公司有多少員工嗎？

🔖 Do you have any recent graduates from _____ University working for you?

有剛從 _____ 大學畢業的學生在　貴公司工作嗎？

🔖 How will employees' performance be evaluated?

公司會如何評估員工的表現？

🔖 How would you describe the atmosphere of your company?

您會如何描述　貴公司的風氣？

🔖 Will I have an opportunity to visit the department and take a look at the facilities?

我是否有機會可以參觀一下　貴部門和設施？

🔖 What type of career paths do people typically follow within this organization?

一般而言，員工的職業階梯如何？

Is the sales growth in the new product line sustainable?

新產品線的銷售狀況持續成長嗎？

Have any new product lines/services/curricula been announced recently?

最近有沒有宣佈任何新的產品線 / 服務 / 課程？

Do your employees work long hours and weekends?

您的員工是否需要長時間工作？週末需要工作嗎？

In your opinion, why is this company a good place to work?

對您而言，為何這間公司是一個工作的好地方？

Have there been any layoffs or restructurings recently?

最近有裁員或重組嗎？

What major challenges is your company currently facing?

貴公司目前所面臨的主要挑戰是甚麼？

How much independence is allowed in dress and appearance?

貴公司在服裝儀容上有多大尺度的自由？

Are there dress codes for work that I should be aware of?

公司對員工的穿著有甚麼要求？

Are there any perks and benefits associated with this job? Like, are there any year-end bonuses(年終獎金) or transportation benefits（交通福利）？

這工作有甚麼福利和津貼嗎？例如，有年終獎金嗎？

求職相關的問題

How long ago was this company established?
貴公司是多久以前成立的？

May I have a copy of the job description, please?
可以給我一份工作內容說明嗎？

Do you expect your sales to keep growing in the coming year?
您認為公司下年的銷售量會持續增長嗎？

How are promotions handled? Is it possible to transfer from one division to another?
升職一般如何處理？是否有部門調職的可能？

How would you describe the management style of the organization?
您會如何描述公司的管理風格？

What is the greatest challenge facing the company?
公司面臨的最大挑戰是甚麼？

What are the company's goals for the upcoming year?
公司來年的目標是甚麼？

How is success in this job measured by the organization?
這項工作是否成功取決於甚麼？

詢問「有關應聘職位的資訊」

1-6.1-02

What would be my priorities for the first month?
我第一個月的工作重點是甚麼？

May I know what a typical first assignment would be?

剛開始會做怎樣的工作呢？

What is the toughest time of year for an employee in the job? Why?

對於員工來說，一年中最艱難的時期是？為甚麼？

What is the top priority for someone in this job?

從事這項工作的人的首要任務是甚麼？

If anyone has failed at this job, why did they fail? What mistakes did they make?

之前有人在這份工作上失敗了嗎？是甚麼導致他們失敗了？他們犯了甚麼錯誤？

What do you expect the person in this job to accomplish in the first year?

您期望這職位的員工於首年達到甚麼目標？

What are the main duties of your team?

您的團隊的主要工作內容是甚麼？

What is the key to success in this job?

這份工作的成功關鍵是甚麼？

Can you give me an example of a great employee success?

您能舉一個員工取得巨大成功的例子嗎？

How much travel is required for this position?

這個職位需要出差嗎？

Are business trips frequently required in this position?

這個職位需要經常出差嗎？

求職相關的問題

Is there anything I could do that would make me more qualified for this position?

為了符合這項工作的必備條件，有甚麼我可以做的嗎？

What is the most important responsibility of this position?

這個職位最重要的責任是甚麼？

What skills and experience would make someone successful in this job?

有甚麼技能和經驗可以使員工成功完成這工作？

How much contact and exposure to management is there?

大概多久跟管理階層接觸一次？

What is the normal routine of a _____ like?

_____的日常業務內容是甚麼？

To whom does the position report?

這個職位的主管是誰？

What do you feel are the most important aspects of this position?

您認為這個職位最重要的是甚麼？

How important is this position within the company?

這項職務在公司的重要性有多高？

Can you describe the corporate culture?

您能描述一下企業文化嗎？

How does the company measure performance?

公司如何衡量員工表現？

詢問「有關應聘公司的內部培訓」

1-6.1-03

📌 What type of training programs do you have?

公司會提供甚麼類型的培訓課程？

📌 What type of orientation programs do you have?

貴公司有甚麼新進職員訓練課程？

📌 What learning opportunities are there?

公司會提供甚麼學習機會？

📌 How many employees go through your training program each year?

每年有多少員工參加公司的培訓計劃？

📌 As you mentioned just now, all new members are required to join training program. When does the training program begin?

正如您剛才提到的，所有新入職的員工都必須參與公司的培訓計劃。請問培訓計劃何時開始？

📌 What type of training programs do you have?

訓練課程有哪些種類？

📌 What other opportunities are available for staff development?

還有甚麼活動可有助員工發展嗎？

📌 Do you offer continuing education and professional training?

公司會提供持續教育或專業訓練嗎？

求職相關的問題

Does your company have formal training programs, or do employees receive on-the-job training? Who is eligible?

貴公司是否有正式的培訓計劃？員工需要接受在職培訓嗎？誰有資格參與？

詢問「有關應聘職位的升職安排」

1-6.1-04

Can I progress at my own pace, or is the career path structured?

升職快慢是依個人進度決定，還是公司方面已有規定？

What is the average time it takes to be promoted to _____(position)?

升職至 _____（職位名稱）層平均需要多久的年資？

What is the typical career path in this area of specialization? How long does it usually take to move from one step to the next in this career path?

在這個專業領域中，典型的晉升階梯如何？在這晉升階梯上，要從一個階段步入下一個階段通常需要多長時間？

What can I expect in terms of job progression in your organization?

貴公司升職方面的情況如何？

In general, are senior jobs filled by experienced people from outside?

一般而言，高級職位是否從公司外部聘請經驗豐富的人擔任？

What percentage of supervisory positions are filled from within the company?

從公司內部提拔的主管比例有多少？

詢問「面試後續」

1-6.1-05

最後，假如你很希望快點得知面試結果，也不要過於直接地問 "When will I know the result?"，以免顯得太心急。這時，你可能婉轉一點問：

What are the next steps in the interview process?

面試的下一步會怎樣安排？

How soon do you want an employee in place?

您希望員工能夠多快入職？

Do you feel I have the characteristics necessary to be hired and to advance in this organization?

您認為我是否具備應聘　貴公司和晉升所必需的特徵？

此外，為表現自己的真心和熱情，你可以再次詢問面試官自己是否需要提供甚麼額外的資料：

Is there anything else I can provide that would be helpful?

我需要提供其他資料給您參閱嗎？

求職相關的問題

小貼士

1 避免問到招聘廣告中已經列出的項目。

2 切忌「無事找事問」。假如你提前預備好的問題已經在與面試官對答中得到答案,那麼,在最後的問答環節時你就不要再問這道問題了。否則,這會顯得你面試不留心,對工作不上心。

3 最好避免詢問有關薪資的問題。若是準備好的問題在面試中已經得到解答,還是建議 play it by ear(隨機應變),即使只有一個問題也好,積極提問才是上策。

4 切忌問太多問題
很多人都以為問題問得愈多,就愈能讓對方感覺到自己的誠意。事實上,這只會使面試官不耐煩,甚至打亂了對方的 schedule。因此,問問題記得「貴精不貴多」,數量應該控制在一至兩個左右。問題要經過篩選再提出,最緊要「精闢簡練、言之有物」。

07 面試後續——撰寫 Thank-you Email

不少求職者都認為在完成面試之後就可以「鬆一口氣」，認為已經「播種施肥」，是回家坐等收成的時候。然而，面試完畢之後真的只能「坐定定」等通知？面試結束後到底能做些甚麼來提高錄取的機率？針對這個問題，網絡上流傳着各種說法，網民們提出的建議千奇百怪、五花八門，我們大致可將他們分為贊成派與反對派。

贊成要「做些甚麼」的網民認為此舉對求職成功有所幫助，有些人提議寫 thank-you email（感謝函）、卡片，甚至還要送禮物；而反對的一方則認為這些舉動不太合適，或這些行為根本無補於事，實為「多此一舉」。那麼面試後到底是否要做些甚麼？而具體又可以做些甚麼呢？

根據各大求職論壇及調查報告的建議，在面試後的黃金 24 小時內向面試官發送一封 thank-you email 其實有助提升對方對你的印象，從而增加錄取機會（注意：切忌「擦鞋」，否則容易弄巧反拙，最終枉費心機）。你可以視發送這封信函為「最後一擊」，把握最後機會讓對方記起你在

面試中的表現，以達到再度自我行銷的效果。另一方面，這封後續的 thank-you email，還能讓面試官感受到你的誠意，更能凸顯你是個有始有終的人，有做好後續追蹤工作的自覺性。

因此，大家不妨在面試後嘗試向面試官發送一封 thank-you email，切記要在面試後的黃金 24 小時內完成發送，如果逾時發送，對方收到後有機會感到「一頭霧水」，甚至會認為你做事欠缺效率、凡事「慢半拍」，最終適得其反。

7.1 如何撰寫 Thank-you Email

撰寫 Thank-you Email 的步驟如下：

第一步	• 在 Email 開首感謝對方給予面試的機會
第二步	• 對藉由面試所認識的工作內容及業界情況等表示興趣或表達對工作的熱忱
第三步	• 再次強調與工作相關的資格及經歷 + 推銷自己（略略帶過，切忌太 over）
第四步	• 表達期盼對方聯絡自己

以下是針對這四大步驟的常用句：

感謝對方給予面試的機會

It was very enjoyable to speak with you about the customer service ambassador position at（company's name）.

我很高興能與您談談　貴公司客戶服務大使一職。

I sincerely enjoyed meeting with you yesterday and learning more about the sales representative position at（company's name）.

我很高興昨天能與您會面，並了解更多有關　貴公司銷售代表職位的資料。

I would like to thank you for the interview and tour of your company yesterday.

感謝您昨天的面談及　貴公司安排的參觀。

Thank you for taking the time to meet me yesterday.

感謝您昨天抽空與我見面。

It was a pleasure meeting with you to discuss career opportunities at（company's name）.

今天能夠與您談到關於　貴公司的工作機會，我深感榮幸。

Thank you for meeting with me this afternoon to discuss the vacancy for a marketing assistant.

感謝您今天下午能夠針對營銷助理一職與我討論。

求職相關的問題

🖈 I enjoyed meeting you and learning more about (company's name).

我非常高興能夠獲得面試機會，以及能對 貴公司有進一步的認識。

🖈 Thank you very much for taking the time to show me around and answering my questions.

感謝您抽空帶我參觀 貴公司並解答我的疑惑。

重申自己對工作的熱忱

🖈 Our conversation confirmed my interest in becoming part of (company's name).

與您談話後，我更肯定自己真的很希望能成為 貴公司的一分子。

🖈 The innovative approach which you described confirmed my desire to work with you.

您所描述的創新方法讓我更加肯定希望與您合作。

🖈 I felt a wonderful rapport with you. Besides, I am more convinced that I will fit in well as a member of the team and will quickly be able to contribute to (company's name).

我相信自己能與您融洽相處。此外，我更加有信心自己能成為團隊中的一員，並能夠迅速貢獻 貴公司。

🖈 To be frank, I am impressed by your (e.g. company culture).

坦白說，我對 貴公司的（公司文化）印象很深刻。

📌 I am impressed with your company's strong marketing plans and strategies for achieving its objectives.

對於 貴公司為達目標所擬定的行銷計劃及策略，我深感敬佩。

📌 I found the questions we discussed just now to be very engaging, and it was exciting to be able to meet the team - a very knowledgeable and friendly group of people.

我發現我們剛才所討論的問題非常引人入勝。能夠與如此知識淵博且友好的團隊會面，實在令人興奮。

再次推銷自己

📌 I am confident that my experiences would enable me to fullfill the job requirements effectively.

我相信我的經驗能夠有效地滿足工作要求。

📌 In addition to my enthusiasm, I will also bring to the position a strong commitment to high quality work, a positive attitude and the ability to encourage others to work cooperatively.

除了熱情外，我還能為公司帶來追求高質量工作的精神、積極的態度和鼓勵他人合作的能力。

📌 I believe that my academic training at the xxx University and my experience working in the International Trade Headquarters at L & Y Corporation qualify me for the position.

我深信在 xxx 大學所受的教育，以及在 L & Y 公司國際貿易總部的工作經驗，能使我勝任這份工作。

求職相關的問題

The job, as you presented it, seems to be a very good match for my skills and interests.

正如您介紹的那樣，這份工作與我的技能和興趣似乎非常吻合。

After meeting you and getting a better understanding of what is involved in the position, I am even more confident that there can be no better match.

與您會面後，加上更深入地了解該職位所涉及的內容後，我更加相信沒有比　貴公司更適合我的公司了。

表達期盼對方聯絡自己

Again, thank you very much for your time and for your consideration.

再次感謝您的寶貴時間和考慮。

Please feel free to contact me if I can provide you with any further information.

如果您需要我提供更多資料，請隨時與我聯繫。

I appreciate the time you and your team took to talk with me. I look forward to hearing from you soon.

感謝您和您的團隊能抽空與我會面。我盼望能盡快收到您的消息。

I would like to meet with you again to further discuss this position.

希望能再次會面，以針對這份工作進行更深入的討論。

📌 I look forward to hearing from you, and thank you again for the courtesy you extended to me.

期盼得到您的回音，在此，再次感謝您的盛情。

📌 I look forward to hearing from you soon regarding your final decision. Feel free to reach out to me beforehand with any questions or concerns. Again, my phone number is 9123-4567.

我期待着您的最終決定。如有任何問題或疑慮，請隨時與我聯繫。我的電話號碼是 9123-4567。

> **範例**

Thank-you Email 範例

Dear Mr. Lau,

It was a pleasure to finally meet you after our many emails and phone conversations regarding the **Sales Representative**（銷售代表）position at L & Y Collection LTD. I appreciate your time and consideration in interviewing me for this position.

Our conversation confirmed my interest in becoming part of your organization. I was particularly pleased with the **innovative**（創新的）**marketing strategies**（營銷策略）you mentioned. Besides, thank you so much for introducing me to several members of your sales team – a very **knowledgeable**（學識淵博）and friendly group of people. Please let them know I appreciate how comfortable they made me feel.

After speaking with you and the sales team, I am confident that I would be a perfect candidate for this position. In addition to my enthusiasm, I can also bring to the position a **strong commitment**（堅定的承諾）to high quality work, a positive attitude and the ability to encourage others to work cooperatively.

I am very interested in working for you and look forward to hearing from you once the final decisions are made regarding this position. Feel free to reach out to me beforehand with any questions or concerns. Again, my phone number is 9123-4567.

Best regards,

(Your Name)

小貼士

寫 Thank-you Email 的時候，要非常小心，切忌有「過度逢迎討好」的感覺。這封信的重點是「表達感謝＋強調你適合這份工作」，而不是「擦靚對方對鞋」。

錯誤示範

This is the best company in the world.

這是世界上最好的公司。

Believe me. You cannot find anyone better than me.

相信我，你找不到比我更好的人了。

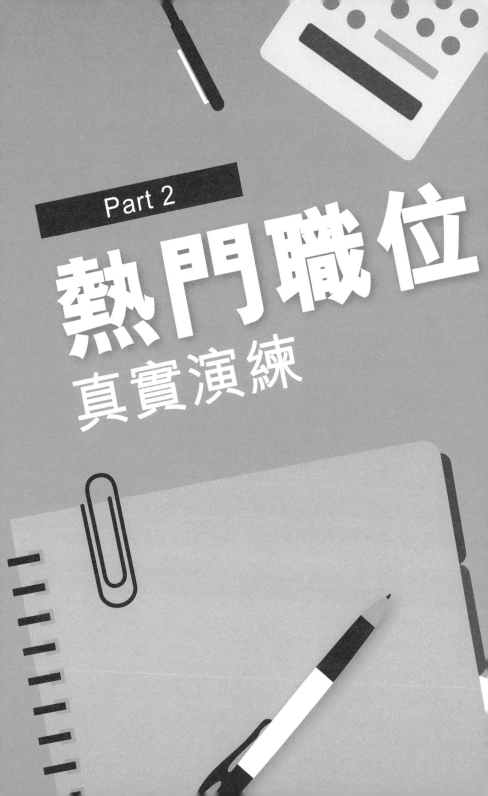

Part 2

熱門職位
真實演練

筆者在前文用了不少的篇幅和大家講解怎樣編寫求職信和履歷表等，好讓大家能順利取得一個面試的機會。此外，又和大家分享了如何回答一些在各種求職面試中經常出現的提問，讓大家可以在面試之前好好裝備自己，並在面試當中讓面試官眼前一亮。

然而，在面試中面試官所提出的問題卻會因工種而異。面試官會根據不同行業或是不同職位的特質和需要，具針對性的設計一系列的問題，並在面試中向面試者提問及留意面試者怎樣應對，並根據他們的反應和表現，篩選出能勝任有關職位的人選。

相信看到這裏的你們，都各自有想投身的行業，在面試時都有機會遇上不同的一套面試問題。為了更貼合大家的需要，筆者精心挑選了幾個熱門的職位，並為每一種職位準備了一些情景會話，讓有意投身這些行業的你們能事先做好準備，提前了解將會遇到一些怎樣的面試情景，或是怎樣的提問。

筆者明白，其實許多人對「面試」充滿恐懼，而當中不少人更因為不善於應對面試，而一次又一次的與心儀的職位擦肩而過。

正所謂「熟能生巧」，筆者特別希望這類人可以多參考以下部分的內容，並且嘗試利用有關的情景會話內容多加練習，克服自己的「恐懼」，在未來的面試中打一場漂亮仗。

說到這裏，筆者想起了一句勵志的名言佳句：「準備種子，就收穫果實；準備努力，就收穫成功；準備今天，就收穫明天。」。人各有志，無論大家想投身哪一個行業，都希望大家可以盡力為心儀的職位好好裝備自己，並憑藉努力在有關行業當中順利取得一席。

接下來的部分將針對不同職業作分類，並分別為「市場營銷」、「餐飲業」、「接待員」、「秘書」、「辦公室文員 / 白領」、「地產 / 保險經紀」、「銷售員」等 7 個熱門的工種介紹相關的面試情景會話內容，方便有意欲應聘有關職位的你們作參考之用。

熱門職位真實演練

營銷行業看重經驗和實力，而非單靠學歷、背景。營銷人員需要做的工作包括「市場調查」、「客戶分析」、「產品設計」、「品牌設計」、「價格制定」、「整合傳播」等。所以，面試的時候要表現自己有信心做好營銷、懂得基本的營銷思路、關注社會熱門話題，並善於把握消費者的心理、勇於接受變化，這樣才能説服面試官自己能做好營銷。

面試「市場營銷」崗位真實演練

About the Job Seeker （求職者）	About the Interviewer （面試官）
Janice Wong	Marcus Lau
holds a BBA in Marketing and Operations Management （市場營銷和運營管理工商管理學士學位）	HR Manager of HkTech, a leading telecom carrier in Hong Kong （香港領先的電信運營商）
has 1 year of relevant work experience	

Marcus	Welcome to HKTech. Janice. I am Marcus.
Janice	Hello, it's nice to meet you.
Marcus	Nice to meet you too. How are you doing today?

3-1-01

Janice	I am doing well, thanks.
Marcus	Great. I hope we didn't keep you waiting for long just now?
Janice	No, I had the chance to talk to one of your sales representatives while waiting.
Marcus	That's good. Janice, shall we start?
Janice	Yes, sure.
Marcus	Okay, let me introduce myself. I'm the HR manager here and we now have an open position, so we have been interviewing applicants to fill the Marketing Assistant position as quickly as possible. Can you briefly introduce yourself?
Janice	Sure. As a graduate of ABC University majoring in Marketing and Operations Management, **I have a passion for problem-solving, collaborating in a group environment**, and taking initiative. After graduating, I developed my skills as a Digital Marketing Assistant for a nonprofit where I updated Facebook and Instagram.

〔描述自己上一份工作的成就〕：While managing the Instagram account, I raised the followers count from 140 to 1,200 and increased the brand awareness beyond Facebook and Instagram.

Besides, I always had **to work under intense pressure**, sell products and services to customers from all backgrounds, handle customer complaints and solve problematic situations. I believe I would be a good fit for the role owing to my **comprehensive** imagination, creativity, and technical **expertise**. I'd describe myself as a **methodical** person as I take care of my work well. I'm also **an analytical problem solver** with **a creative edge** and a passion for technology, innovation and people.

I have a passion for… 熱衷於……．

problem-solving 解決問題

collaborating in a group environment 在小組環境中合作

熱門職位真實演練

to work under intense pressure 在巨大的壓力下工作
comprehensive 全面的
expertise 專長
methodical 有條理的
an analytical problem solver 分析型問題解決者
a creative edge 創造力

Marcus   That's good to hear. Why do you think you are the right fit for this role? I mean, why should we hire you?

Janice   I'm confident that I'm **an excellent** fit with your company. I know that there may be others with similar abilities, but I have something they may not have. I have **an attitude for excellence**, and **an infectious desire** to assisting with promotional activities. Besides, I am a **highly motivated**, **result-oriented** individual, who is willing to **go an extra mile** to reach goals and learn along the way. For example, my previous job involved meeting specific targets on a daily basis, which I managed and sometimes **surpassed** while gaining **better means** of improving the achievement of those goals. I'm confident that if given this opportunity, I will **thrive** and deliver quality work **within stipulated deadlines**. I look forward to contributing my creativity, marketing and organizational skills and experiences to HKTech.

an excellent fit 非常適合
an attitude for excellence 追求卓越的態度
an infectious desire 極強的感染力
highly motivated 積極進取
result-oriented 重視結果的
go an extra mile 付出更多的努力
surpassed 超越
better means 更佳的方法
thrive 蓬勃發展
within stipulated deadlines 規定的期限內

Marcus   Very well. Have you ever participated in any **marketing campaigns**?

marketing campaigns 營銷活動

Janice	Yes, in my previous role as a Marketing Assistant, I had to help initiate a series of marketing campaigns including print, **digital**, and **social media analysis**, and content for direct mail campaigns and blogs.

digital 電子的
social media analysis 社交媒體分析

Marcus	That's good. Now, for social media marketing, which social media channel do you prefer and why?
Janice	（小貼士：回答時，要結合專業概念並加入自己的理解，最好還能使用相關示例來豐富答案。）

To me, **every** social media platform **has its advantages**. Plus, they **represent** different audiences. I **tend to vary** my approach based on the product or service and the target consumer. Let's say, if we are targeting **the younger generations**, I may favor platforms that **resonate with** the under-30 group, like Instagram and Youtube. In fact, Facebook and YouTube are both excellent additions for reaching nearly any age group since they rate the highest **in overall usage**.

every＿＿＿has its advantages 每個 ＿＿＿ 都有其優勢
represent 代表
tend to 傾向於
vary 改變
resonate with 與……產生共鳴
the younger generations 年輕的幾代人
in overall usage 總體使用上

Marcus	I agree. Now, have you heard of our company's mission?
Janice	Yes, I read HKTech's **mission** and vision. After finding out more information about your company from social media, I can clearly see how my goals align with the purposes of the company., HKTech's mission to be the first-choice digital marketing partner providing 360-degree **marketing services** to businesses is **inspiring**, and I would

熱門職位真實演練

be **thrilled** to be able **to contribute** to this mission. There's nothing I love more than when I am working with other engaged individuals towards a common goal, and that's what excited me about working here.

mission 使命
marketing services 營銷服務
inspiring 鼓舞人心的
thrilled 激動；興奮
to contribute 貢獻

Marcus   I'm glad that you've done some research before coming to here. Can you tell me what your greatest strength is?

Janice   Sure. I have strong organization skills and am good at **strategically** thinking through business issues to help grow the company.

〔提供相關示例來豐富答案〕：For example, a few months ago, my marketing manager wanted me to prepare some social media graphics for four different campaigns in the same month. I was responsible for delivering and posting around 8 to 10 graphics per week. **To keep track of** my progress, I made one **main folder** on **Google Drive** and created **sub-folders** for each campaign. I was able to meet all the deadlines that were set **on a weekly basis**.

strategically 有策略地；戰略性地
to keep track of... 為了跟進 ……
Google Drive 雲端硬碟
main folder 主文件夾
sub-folders 子文件夾
on a weekly basis 每週

Marcus   Then, what's your greatest weakness?

Janice   （小貼士：當被問到自己最大的弱點是甚麼時，第一步是「真誠地暴露自己的弱點」，第二步是「主動提供針對這弱點的解決方案」或「展示自己正為此弱點作出最大努力去改善」。）

When I'm too excited or **anxious**, I talk very fast. To **overcome** this, I remind myself to take a deep breath, **address** my pace, and slow down. I've learned to **replenish** my breath by pausing **occasionally**, every 6 to 8 words.

anxious 焦慮
overcome 克服
to address 注意；解決
to replenish 補充
occasionally 偶爾

Marcus   Well...I used to talk very fast too when I was a student. To cope with this problem, I practiced calming myself down so that I can slow down the rhythm of my speech. Now, if you want me to talk slower, I can talk slower. If you want me to talk faster, I can speed up a bit. You can also record yourself speaking as it will help you identify places you should slow down.

Janice   （小貼士：假如面試官為你提供了有用的意見，記得誠懇地答謝對方，以示尊重。）

Thank you so much for your suggestions. I will definitely try them out at home.

Marcus   Great. Now, I have the last question for you. What are your career aspirations?

Janice   Well...when I think of my career aspirations, I think of a timeframe maybe 5 years from now. After researching your company and learning more about this position, I feel that this role fits well with my future aspirations. I'd love **to assume more responsibilities** and get involved in marketing strategy. **Ultimately**, my goal would be **to embrace** platforms that the target market connects with because that allows us **to showcase** a product or service in a place they already frequent. I believe that can **create the widest reach**. Besides, as far as I know, your company has a number of critical clients who are taken

Part 2

熱門職位真實演練

care of by only your **top marketers**. My career goal in the coming 5 years is to become part of that marketing team.

Marcus   Very well, Janice. Is there anything you would like to ask me?

Janice   Yes, I'd like to know a little bit more about HKTech. Have any new product lines or services been announced recently?

Marcus   Recently, we are planning to launch a new data plan package to take advantage of the power of 5G. If we set the regular price of the plan at HKD$369 per month, which includes 100GB 5G local data, is it attractive to customers?

（小貼士：要有心理準備面試官有可能會就着你詢問的問題來問你一些 follow-up questions。）

Janice   As far as I know, the price of other similar packages in the same industry is HKD$350-450. To attract more customers, maybe we can launch **a limited time period offer** in which users can get an extra data, let's say 20GB, with its **prepaid annual plan**.

Marcus   Thank you, Janice. It's been good talking to you. I can tell that you are a good candidate. Expect to hear from us within a week or so.

Janice   Nice meeting you too. Thank you for your time.

Marcus   Thanks for coming to the interview. Goodbye.

Janice   Goodbye.

求職英語一本通

可能遇到的面試問題

3-1-02

📌 Tell me how you got started in your career.
告訴我你的職業生涯是如何開始的。

📌 What do you think are the three essential skills for a career in marketing?
你認為營銷職業的三項基本技能是甚麼？

📌 How familiar are you with our target market?
你對我們的目標市場有多熟悉？

📌 What makes you passionate about this work?
是甚麼讓你對這項工作充滿熱情？

📌 How has your skillset grown over time?
隨着時間的推移，你的技能發展如何？

📌 What inspired you to pursue a career in marketing?
是甚麼激發了你從事市場營銷職業的？

📌 What other companies are you interviewing for?
你還有在哪些公司面試？

📌 How did you learn about this open position?
你是如何得知這個空缺職位的？

📌 What can you tell me about our company?
你能說出有關我們公司的甚麼訊息？

📌 What kind of management style do you prefer?
你喜歡哪種管理風格？

📌 Why are you leaving your current position?
你為甚麼要離開現在的職位？

What do you consider to be your core strengths?
你認為你的核心優勢是甚麼？

Who's your favorite marketer and why?
誰是你最喜歡的營銷人員，為甚麼？

In your own words, what's the goal of marketing?
營銷的目標是甚麼？請用自己的文字表達。

How would you manage a new product launch?
你一般如何管理新產品的發佈？

Chapter 09 餐飲業

面試「餐飲業」崗位真實演練

About the Job Seeker （求職者）	About the Interviewer （面試官）
📌 Kimmy Liu 📌 holds a Diploma in Catering with Event Management（餐飲與活動管理文憑） 📌 has 1 year of relevant work experience	📌 Pablo Marcela 📌 Restaurant Manager of Momento Festivo, A Spanish Michelin restaurant（西班牙米芝蓮餐廳）

Pablo   Welcome to Momento Festivo, Kimmy. I am Pablo Marcela.

Kimmy   Hello, Mr. Marcela. It's nice to meet you.

Pablo   Nice to meet you too. How are you doing today?

3-2-01

Kimmy   I am doing well, thanks.

Pablo   That's good. Kimmy, shall we start?

Kimmy   Yes, sure.

Pablo   Okay, let me introduce myself first. I'm the restaurant manager here and we have been interviewing applicants recently as we are in need of three waiters or waitresses as quickly as possible **to cope with demand**. Kimmy, I noticed that you just graduated last year. Do you have any relevant experience with working in catering?

to cope with demand 應付需求

熱門職位真實演練

Kimmy	Yes, I have one-year full-time experience as a waitress at a local hotel. I also worked as a part-time waitress at a **western restaurant** during my two-year diploma program.

western restaurant 西餐廳

Pablo	Very well, Kimmy. I'd like to know more about your experience working as a waitress at a local hotel. Can you describe your previous duties?

Kimmy	Sure. In my previous experience, I had to **serve** afternoon tea and formal dining, handle food and **beverage** orders at a good pace, **arrange table settings**, make suggestions based on guests' **preferences**, cooperate and communicate with all **serving** and **kitchen staff**, and **adhere to** all relevant **health department regulations** and **customer service guidelines**. I learned food handling skills and some safety issues as well.

serve 服務
beverage 飲料
arrange table settings 安排餐桌設置
preferences 偏好；喜好
serving staff 在職工作人員
kitchen staff 廚房工作人員
adhere to 遵守
health department regulations 衛生部門規定
food handling skills 食品處理技巧
customer service guideline 客戶服務準則

Pablo	How do you perceive **food handling**?

food handling 食物處理

Kimmy	As a waitress, it's my **responsibility** to **abide by** government **food safety** and **public health guidelines**. If necessary, **catering staff members** have to wear **protective gear** or use certain **food storing methods**. I agree that health and safety is a **priority**, and I am **committed to** keeping a clean and **sanitary** environment at work.

responsibility 責任
abide by 遵守

food safety guidelines 食品安全準則
public health guidelines 公共衛生準則
catering staff members 餐飲工作人員
protective gear 防護裝備
food storing methods 食物儲存方法
priority 優先事項
be committed to 致力於
sanitary 清潔衛生的

Pablo   Wonderful. Kimmy, why do you think you are a good fit?

Kimmy   <u>First of all</u>, I'm **highly motivated** and being part as a team is my **passion**. I deliver in my service both for **guest satisfaction** and the company I work for. As a waitress, I strive for complete customer satisfaction and the best customer service. I believe that in all **professions**, **giving 100%** is always **necessary**. <u>Secondly</u>, I **adapt** quickly since I am **a fast learner**. I'd love **to spread my knowledge** and continue to grow as a team member and work really hard at all times to achieve my goals in the catering industry. <u>Thirdly</u>, I'm **strong minded** and always focused on the right things and listen to my managers so I can grow to be like them. I believe I have the catering experience, **ambition**, and drive you are looking for. I am confident that I would make a valuable addition to Momento Festivo.

highly motivated 上進心強
passion 熱情
guest satisfaction 賓客滿意度
professions 職業
giving 100% 付出 100%的努力
necessary 必要的
adapt 適應
a fast learner 快速的學習者
to spread my knowledge 傳播我的知識
strong minded 意志堅定；胸懷開闊
ambition 雄心壯志

熱門職位真實演練

Pablo	Do you know anything about our restaurant?
Kimmy	As far as I know, Momento Festivo is a Spanish **Michelin star restaurant** which aims to provide high quality, **authentic** and traditional Spanish food in a relaxed environment. Your restaurant is not only famous for your excellent **cuisine** like **seafood paella** and **gazpacho**, but also famous for your **Signature Tortilla de patatas**, a traditional Spanish dish presented in a modern way by your **executive chef** Tamara Agustín, who was directly recruited from Madrid.

highly motivated 上進心強
Michelin star restaurant 米芝蓮星級餐廳
authentic 真正的；地道的
cuisine 美食；佳餚
seafood paella 西班牙海鮮飯
gazpacho 西班牙涼菜湯
Signature 招牌的
Tortilla de patatas 墨西哥玉米餅
executive chef 行政總廚

Pablo	I'm glad that you've done some research before coming to here. Now, Kimmy, I'd like to know whether you are good at remember the names of dishes. As you know, this is a Spanish restaurant; nearly all of our dishes are named in Spanish.
Kimmy	I'm actually quite familiar with Spanish dishes as I'm so into the Spanish culture. I've also learned a bit Spanish with my Mexican friends. Plus, as I mentioned, I'm **a fast learner**. That's why I'm confident that I can remember the names of your dishes successfully and start taking orders and serving food to your guests within the first week of my work. **I'm devoted to** taking every customer through a journey in **Spanish culinary tradition**.

a fast learner 善於學習的人
be devoted to 致力於
Spanish culinary tradition 西班牙的烹飪傳統

Pablo	Great, Kimmy. Now, I have a last question for you. What are your salary expectations?
Kimmy	From the research that I have done, it appears to be in the HKD15,000 to HKD18,000 range. Is that the range you had in mind?
Pablo	Well, the **minimum salary** we offer for this position is HKD15,500 gross per month for full-time. The **actual salary** will **depend on** relevant experience and qualification of the designated candidate and will be negotiated at the time of the job offer.

minimum salary 最低薪資
actual salary 實際工資
depend on 取決於

Kimmy	Basically, the salary you provide is in line with my expectations. I look forward to discussing in more detail what my responsibilities at your restaurant would be. From there, we can determine **a fair salary** for the position.

a fair salary 合理的薪水

Pablo	Good. Kimmy, is there anything you would like to ask me?
Kimmy	Do you offer continuing education and **professional training**?

professional training 專業訓練

Pablo	Yes, as you know, our restaurant aims to provide high quality service to our guests. Therefore, to ensure that our staff are trained effectively, every new hire is required to join a training programme. More information will be given to you if you are hired.
Kimmy	Thank you so much for providing information on this. It sounds amazing. I'm confident that if given this opportunity, I will thrive and can contribute my **catering skills** and experiences to Momento Festivo.

catering skills 餐飲技巧

Pablo	Thank you, Kimmy. It's been good talking to you. I can tell that you are a good candidate. Expect to hear from us within a week or so.

Kimmy	Nice meeting you too. Thank you for your time. I'm looking forward to hearing about the next steps, and don't hesitate to contact me if you have any questions or concerns in the meantime.
Pablo	Sure. Thanks for coming to the interview. Goodbye.
Kimmy	Goodbye.

可能遇到的面試問題

3-2-02

🚩 What is your availability?
你甚麼時候方便上班？

🚩 Imagine that there is insufficient food for the guests in the restaurant. What will you do?
想像一下，假如餐廳沒有足夠的食物提供給客人。你會怎樣做？

🚩 What will you do to ensure that the food items are not damaged during the transportation to the venue?
你如何確保食品在運送期間不會損壞？

🚩 Do you consider yourself a team player?
你認為自己是否團隊合作者？

🚩 The evening has ended, and the last guest has left the restaurant. Explain the duties you will take care of before leaving the venue.
晚餐結束了，最後一位客人也離開餐廳了。在離開會場之前，你有甚麼需要處理？

🚩 Tell me how you got started in your career.
告訴我你的職業生涯是如何開始的。

What makes you passionate about this work?
是甚麼讓你對這項工作充滿熱情？

What experience do you have in catering?
你在餐飲方面有甚麼經驗？

How do you handle difficult customers?
你如何處理麻煩的顧客？

Do you enjoy working within a team?
你喜歡團隊工作嗎？

Why do you want to work for us?
為甚麼你想在我們的餐廳工作？

What can you tell me about our company?
你能説出有關我們公司的甚麼訊息？

Why are you leaving your current position?
你為甚麼要離開現在的職位？

What do you consider to be your core strengths?
你認為你的核心優勢是甚麼？

How would you handle a difficult guest?
面對麻煩的客人，你會如何處理？

What is your food handling experience?
你有甚麼食品處理經驗？

What are your career goals in the catering industry?
你在餐飲業的職業目標是甚麼？

What are your salary expectations?
你的預期薪水是多少？

What do you think could be challenging in this position?
你認為在這個職位上有甚麼是具有挑戰性的？

Part 2

熱門職位真實演練

接待員（Receptionist）一般負責執行行政和辦公任務，例如接聽電話、回覆電子郵件、接待訪客，並向公眾和客戶提供有關其組織的一般訊息。接待員在任何公司中都佔據着關鍵和可靠的角色。要駕馭這職位，求職者必須具備強大的組織和溝通技巧，包括客戶服務（Customer Services）、多任務處理（Multitasking）等軟技能，以及能夠快速作出判斷。由於工作場所的技術進步不斷增加，接待員也必須具備一定的技術技能。除了 Microsoft Office 等軟件和行業專用軟件之外，還應具有使用電話系統和辦公設備（如打印機、掃描器和傳真機）的經驗。

面試「接待員」崗位真實演練

About the Job Seeker（求職者）	About the Interviewer（面試官）
Elsa Leung a Form 6 HKDSE graduate with 3 years of relevant work experience （中六文憑試畢業生，具有 3 年相關工作經驗）	Monique Lui HR Manager of Hotel Palace, a five-star hotel in Hong Kong （香港五星級酒店）

求職英語一本通

Monique	Welcome to Hotel Palace, Elsa. I am Monique Lui. You can call me Miss Lui.
Elsa	Hello, Miss Lui. Nice to meet you.
Monique	Nice to meet you too. How are you doing today?
Elsa	I am doing well, thanks.
Monique	That's good. Elsa, shall we start?
Elsa	Yes, sure.
Monique	Okay, let me introduce myself. I'm the HR manager here at Hotel Palace, and we now have an open position, so we have been interviewing applicants to fill the Receptionist position. Can you briefly introduce yourself?
Elsa	Sure. First of all, I have been working as a receptionist for over three years. I'm an **enthusiastic** person who is seeking a new challenging career after my experience as a receptionist at MangoTravel, one of the most **influential** travel **wholesalers** in Hong Kong, and my experience as a receptionist, at a local four-star hotel. With my **negotiation skills**, I have helped MangoTravel **to maximize its profits** by confirming many bookings with **special rates** in a short time. In my experience at the hotel, I have developed good sales experience by promoting specific hotel services and offer suggestions. I believe that my experience working in these two organizations **qualify me for this position**.

3-3-01

enthusiastic 熱情的
influential 具影響力的
wholesalers 批發商
negotiation skills 談判技巧
to maximize its profits 使利潤達到最大化
special rates 特惠價
qualify me for this position 使我有資格擔任這個職位

Monique	Very well, Elsa. I'd like to know more about your experience working as a receptionist at the hotel. Can you describe your previous duties?

Part 2

熱門職位真實演練

Elsa　Yes, of course. In my previous work experience, I was trained to work under high pressure in a **fast-paced** environment. My responsibility included making a smooth check-in and check-out to make sure our guests had a pleasant stay. and **dealing with** sensitive situations. Besides, I was **keen** to support the hotel by maximizing its revenue. For example, I had to promote specific hotel services and offer suggestions. **During my shift**, I had to contact with both local and international guests in person or by phone, so it was important for me to speak in a clear and professional way and **maintain a positive tone**. I was also responsible for dealing with bookings by phone or by email and **allocate** the rooms at the hotel based on the **specific request** of each guest. Indeed, good communication skills and a positive work relation approach also helped me **to excel** at my job.

fast-paced 節奏快的
dealing with 處理
keen 熱衷於
during my shift 輪班期間
maintain a positive tone 保持積極的態度
allocate 分配
specific request 特定要求
to excel 脫穎而出

Monique　Thanks for your sharing, Elsa. Then, what software and hardware do you usually use in terms of office documentation and office administration?

Elsa　I have experience using the full **Microsoft Office suite**, such as Word, Excel, and Access. I also have experience with some **specialized software** like Outlook and Google Drive. I also used Zoom and Microsoft Teams since the start of the **COVID-19 pandemic**. Besides, I'm also familiar with office **equipment**, including **fax machines**, **copiers**, **scanners**, **printers** and telephones.

Microsoft Office suite: Microsoft Office 微軟的辦公軟件套裝
specialized software 專業軟件
COVID-19 pandemic 2019 冠狀病毒病大流行
equipment 設備
fax machines 傳真機
copiers 影印機
scanners 掃描器
printers 打印機

Monique	It seems like you know a lot of things, Elsa.
Elsa	（小貼士：記得要時刻保持謙虛。即使得到面試官的讚賞，也要保持虛心受教的態度。切忌說 "Yes. I really know a lot." 之類的說話。）
	Thank you, Miss Lui. I know that there are still many things I need to learn.
Monique	What do you think is the most essential quality for a receptionist to have?
Elsa	I believe that a great receptionist should be confident with **social interactions** in order to make guests and customers feel comfortable and **at ease**. Also, he or she should also have excellent **organizational skills**. For example, having the ability to find files and phone numbers **at a moment's notice** and **maintain a tidy work area** is very important.
	〔當說到接待人員必須具備的條件時，不妨說說自己的經歷，暗示自己也符合這條件〕：In my previous work experience, I also helped **implement filing systems** so that we could always have the **key contacts at our fingertips**.
	Finally, it's **vital** to make a great **first impression** by keeping a smile because a receptionist is **the first face** of a company.

social interactions 社交互動
at ease 放鬆
organizational skills 組織能力
at a moment's notice 馬上通知
maintain a tidy work area 保持整潔的工作區
implement filing systems 建立歸檔系統

key contacts 常用 / 關鍵聯絡人
at our fingertips 觸手可及；隨時
vital 必不可少的
first impression 第一印象
the first face 第一面

Monique   Yes, you're right. Now, what's your typing speed and error rating?

Elsa   I type English at roughly 80 to 90 **WPM**, and Chinese at around 40 to 50 WPM with a decent level of **accuracy**. I'm very **detail-oriented** and I always ensure my work is carefully **proofread** and edited. I'm also happy to take **an entrance test** if necessary.

WPM=words-per-minute 每分鐘字數
accuracy 準確性
detail-oriented 注重細節
proofread 校對
an entrance test 入職考試

Monique   Okay. How would you manage confidential information?

Elsa   I would make sure that confidential information is protected **in and outside of my workplace**. For example, I'd **ensure** that confidential information **is not left unattended**, particularly in areas which may be **accessible** by the public. I would not give out private information to anyone **unless** that person **has authorized** it in advance.

in and outside of my workplace 在我的工作場所內外
ensure 確保
is not left unattended 無人看管；無人值守
accessible 可以到訪的
unless 除非
has authorized 已授權

Monique   Great, Elsa. Now, I have a last question for you. What languages do you speak?

Elsa   My native language is Cantonese, and I speak fluent English and Mandarin.

Monique   Good. Elsa, do you have anything to ask me?

Elsa	Are there dress codes for work that I should be aware of?
Monique	Yes. Receptionists here have to maintain a proper dress code because, you know, they are the first people a guest or customers sees when walking in. For example, they have to iron their uniform regularly to maintain high level of professionalism. Also, **collared** and **tailored shirts** are encouraged but **fitted shirts**, t-shirts and **sleeveless shirts** are not that appropriate.

collared shirts 有領襯衫
tailored shirts 度身訂造的襯衫
fitted shirts 窄身襯衫
sleeveless shirts 無袖襯衫

Elsa	I see. Thank you so much for your information. I'm used to maintaining a professional attire.
Monique	Wonderful. Thank you, Elsa. It's been good talking to you. I can tell that you are a good candidate. Expect to hear from us within a week or so.
Elsa	Nice meeting you too. Thank you so much for your time.
Monique	Thanks for coming to the interview. Goodbye.
Elsa	Goodbye.

可能遇到的面試問題

3-3-02

Tell me how you got started in your career.
告訴我你的職業生涯是如何開始的。

What makes you passionate about this work?
是甚麼讓你對這項工作充滿熱情？

What can you tell me about our company?
你能說出有關我們公司的甚麼訊息？

Part 2

熱門職位真實演練

Why are you leaving your current position?
你為甚麼要離開現在的職位？

What do you consider to be your core strengths?
你認為你的核心優勢是甚麼？

What programs and software do you have experience using?

你有使用過哪些程式和軟件？

How do you keep your daily schedule organized?
你如何保持每天的日程得以好好安排？

How do you handle a fast-paced work environment?
你如何應對節奏急速的工作環境？

What would your current or previous manager say that you could improve in?

你現任或前任經理有沒有提及過你有甚麼地方需要改進？

How did you ensure that you meet deadlines?
你如何確保任務能按時完成？

What characterize a good receptionist?
一個好的接待員的特徵是甚麼？

Do you have experience maintaining any general office filing system?

你有沒有維護一般辦公室歸檔系統的經驗？

How do you manage your workload when you're really busy?

當你真的很忙時，你會如何管理工作？

What are your most / least favorite things about being a receptionist?

作為接待員，你最喜歡 / 最不喜歡的事情是甚麼？

Describe to me the duties you were responsible for in your last position.

描述你在上一個職位的職責。

What is the extent of your customer service experience?

你的客戶服務經驗如何？

In your opinion, what role does a receptionist play in contributing to office culture?

你認為接待員在促進辦公文化中扮演甚麼角色？

Are you willing to work overtime if necessary?

如有必要，你可以加班嗎？

What experience do you have in handling secure or confidential information?

你在處理安全或機密訊息方面有甚麼經驗？

Can you tell me what attracted you to this company?

你能告訴我甚麼吸引你到這家公司應徵嗎？

作為老闆的得力秘書，你除了要負責每天的行程安排外，還要有心理準備處理大大小小的工作，例如整理和妥善保存主管、老闆交付的文書資料，安排和紀錄會議、處理文書資料、搜集資料、接待貴賓、客戶、支援公司活動、處理雜項事務例如幫老闆斟茶倒水、照顧老闆辦公室的盆栽、整理老闆的辦公桌等。因此，一個好的秘書需要具備以下條件：

- 細心
- 多任務處理能力 (multitasking skills)
- 耐心
- 高情商（EQ）
- 高智商（IQ）
- 守口如瓶
- 具責任感
- 良好的公關能力 (public relations skills)
- 喜愛與人互動
- 良好的溝通協調能力
- 善於跨部門的溝通 (inter-departmental communication)

About the Job Seeker（求職者）

- Isabelle Yip
- holds a Higher Diploma in Corporate Administration（企業管理高級文憑）
- has 1 year of relevant work experience

About the Interviewer（面試官）

- Austin Cook
- HR Manager of The Ads Factory, one of the leading advertising agencies in Hong Kong（香港最頂尖的廣告公司之一）

Austin	Welcome to The Ads Factory, Isabelle. I am Austin Cook.
Isabelle	Hello, it's nice to meet you, Mr. Cook.
Austin	Nice to meet you, too. You can call me Austin. How are you doing today?
Isabelle	I am doing well, thanks.
Austin	That's good, Isabelle. Shall we start?
Isabelle	Yes, sure.
Austin	Alright. Let me introduce myself first. I'm the HR manager here and we now have an open position, so we have been interviewing applicants to fill the Secretary position as quickly as possible. Can you briefly introduce yourself?
Isabelle	Sure. After completing my Higher Diploma in Corporate Administration, I worked as a secretary at **a law firm**. I have been trained to **work under high pressure** in **a fast-paced environment** and work **independently** within a team. In my previous job, I always had **to administer** a number of cases **simultaneously within the requisite time frames**. I am **a good planner** who is good at organizing things and will use **all my potential** to fulfil the same in this industry. I would be proud to build a career with The Ads Factory.

3-4-01

a law firm 律師事務所
work under high pressure 在高壓下工作
a fast-paced environment 節奏急速的環境
independently 獨立地
to administer 處理；管理
simultaneously 同時地
within the requisite time frames 在特定的時間範圍內
a good planner 善於計劃的人
all my potential 我所有的潛力

Austin　Very well, Isabelle. I'd like to know more about your experience working as a secretary at a law firm. Can you describe your previous duties?

Isabelle　At my previous job, I was responsible for managing calendars for **multiple attorneys** by planning and scheduling **conferences, teleconferences**, and business trips. I also had **to compose daily reports** and **routine correspondences**, produce information by **transcribing**, formatting, inputting, editing and **transmitting** data. Besides, I also needed to perform **administrative duties** like operating phone systems, faxing, printing, copying, and mailing.

multiple 多（位）
attorney 律師
conferences 會議
teleconferences 電話會議
to compose daily reports 撰寫每日報告
routine correspondences 例行信函
transcribing 轉錄
transmitting 傳輸
administrative duties 行政職責

Austin　Very well, Isabelle. Now, why do you think you are the right fit for this role? I mean, why should we hire you?

Isabelle　My background experience, as a secretary, **has equipped me** with the relevant skills for this role. Although there may be others with similar abilities, I'm confident that I'm **an excellent fit**

with your organization because I have something they may not have. For example, I have **an attitude for excellence**, and I am a **highly motivated**, **result-oriented** individual, who is willing to **go an extra mile** to reach goals and learn along the way. My previous experience **has entailed** various challenges and **enhanced** my **multitasking skills**. Even when I'm handling a number of tasks at the same time, I'm still keen on maintaining quality and productivity. I'm confident that if given this opportunity, I will **thrive** and deliver quality work **within stipulated deadlines**. I really hope that I can contribute my multitasking and organizational skills and experiences to The Ads Factory.

has equipped me 使我具備了
an excellent fit 非常適合
an attitude for excellence 追求卓越的態度
highly motivated 積極進取
result-oriented 重視結果的
go an extra mile 付出更多的努力
has entailed 帶來了
has enhanced 增強了
multitasking skills 多任務處理能力
thrive 蓬勃發展
within stipulated deadlines 規定的期限內

Austin   Great. May I know the reason why you applied for this secretarial position?

Isabelle   There are four main reasons why I applied for this job. First of all, **the reputation of your company** is certainly a factor. I'd be proud to build a career with The Ads Factory, a company **with such a long history** in the advertising **industry**. Secondly, I know that the culture of your company **supports learning and development on the job** and really rewards hard work. These are **values** I also share and feel I could be an excellent fit with The Ads Factory. Thirdly, I am aware that your company **is passionate about sustainability**, and this was one of the first aspects that attracted me to The Ads Factory. In my previous job, apart from the job duties I mentioned just now, I also **took an active role** in the company's **corporate responsibility**. For example, I tried to source **recyclable** office materials and encouraged everyone in the office to be more **environmentally friendly**. Finally, I consider myself an **innovator** and I'd like to work for a company that's leading the future of the industry.

the reputation of your company 貴公司的聲譽
with such a long history 擁有悠久的歷史
industry 行業
supports learning and development on the job 支持在職學習和發展
values 價值觀
is passionate about... 對……充滿熱情
sustainability 永續性；可持續性
took an active role 積極參與
corporate responsibility 企業責任
recyclable 可回收的
environmentally friendly 環保
innovator 創新者

Austin   It seems like you did enjoy working in your previous company. So why did you quit the job?

Isabelle Well, my former employer **underwent a restructuring** and the secretarial position in the department **had been eliminated. Frankly speaking**, it was a difficult time, but **I left with the confidence** that I had developed important skills there and built strong relationships with my colleagues. I'm now looking forward to the opportunity to apply those experiences in my next job.

underwent a restructuring 重組架構
had been eliminated 被取消
frankly speaking 坦白説
I left with confidence 滿懷信心地

Austin   I see. It's always good to stay positive and think positively. Then, what do you think is your biggest weakness?

Isabelle   （小貼士：當被問到自己最大的弱點是甚麼時，第一步是「真誠地暴露自己的弱點」，第二步是「主動提供針對這弱點的解決方案」或「展示自己正為此弱點作出最大努力去改善」。）

Let me think...well, when I was **a tertiary student**, I was used to coping with **high-pressure** assignments and **meeting strict deadlines**. Therefore, I'm used to **working at high pace**. Sometimes when my colleagues perform tasks at a slower pace than I do, I may feel **frustrated**. But now, I've learned to recognize that everyone has his or her **work standards** and **levels of productivity**. We should **respect** everyone's working style. In my previous job, I was responsible for ensuring all the deadlines were met. In order not **to interrupt** my co-workers **progress** with a visit or a call, I used Smartsheet, **a work-execution** tool **to track** tasks and due dates. For example, I set alerts, updates, and reminders for them.

a tertiary student 大專生
high-pressure 高壓的
meeting strict deadlines 嚴格遵守期限
working at high pace 高速工作
frustrated 沮喪的
work standards 工作標準
levels of productivity 生產力水平
respect 尊重
to interrupt 打斷
progess 進度
a work-execution tool 工作執行工具
to track 追蹤

Austin   Glad to hear that you've figured out how to cope with this weakness. So, how about your biggest strength?

熱門職位真實演練

Isabelle	I believe that my biggest strength **lies in my ability** to adapt to changing situations. When something **unexpected** happens, I readily change gears in response. I am aware that the role of a secretary is a **varied** one and **I pride myself on** being **flexible** and **reliable** with **a 'get-it-done' mentality**.

> lies in my ability to... 在於我 …… 的能力
> unexpected 意料之外
> varied 多種多樣的；多變的
> I pride myself on... 我以自己能 …… 感到驕傲
> flexible 靈活的；有彈性的
> reliable 可靠的
> a 'get it done' mentality 一種「做得到的」的心態

Austin	Right. Having a 'get-it-done' mentality is really important. Now, I have the last question for you, Isabelle. What is your main motivation to succeed at work?
Isabelle	To me, **self-motivation** is **the key to** being a good secretary. As a self-motivated person, I am able **to inspire** myself **constantly** and I always use my **initiative** and flexibility to work independently and in teams to produce **desired results**.

> self-motivation 自我激勵
> the key to _____ …… 的關鍵
> to inspire 啟發
> constantly 不斷地
> initiative 主動性
> desired results 理想的結果

Austin	Good. Isabelle, do you have anything to ask me?
Isabelle	How would you describe the **atmosphere** of your company?

> atmosphere 氛圍

Austin	The Ads Factory **strives to** create a professional and innovative environment while maintaining a family-like atmosphere in which everyone has a place to learn, grow and **excel**. The atmosphere of The Ads Factory would be comfortable.

Isabelle	That's awesome. I always believe that integrating employees into the organization can increase their job satisfaction, thereby yielding the best results.
Austin	Yea, you're right. Okay, Isabelle. I think we have to end here. It's been good talking to you. I can tell that you are a good candidate. Expect to hear from us within a week or so.
Isabelle	Nice meeting you too. Thank you for your time. I'm looking forward to hearing about the next steps, and don't hesitate to contact me if you have any questions or concerns in the meantime.
Austin	Sure. Thanks for coming to the interview. Goodbye.
Isabelle	Goodbye.

可能遇到的面試問題

3-4-02

🔖 Tell me how you got started in your career.
告訴我你的職業生涯是如何開始的。

🔖 What qualities do you consider the most important in a secretarial job?
你認為秘書最重要的質素是甚麼？

🔖 Why should we hire you, and not one of many other candidates who try to get this secretary position?
你認為我們為甚麼要聘用你，而非其他申請這職位的求職者？

🔖 Describe a time when you were faced with a stressful situation.
描述一次你面對壓力的經歷。

Appendix 2 | Appendix 1

Part 2

Part 1

熱門職位真實演練

Tell me about a time that you were not satisfied with your work performance. What did you do about it?

描述一次你對自己工作表現不滿意的經歷。你為此做了甚麼？

Describe a difficult problem you had to sort out in your previous work experience.

描述你在以前的工作經歷中必須解決的一個難題。

Can you work with MS Office?

你懂得使用 MS Office 嗎？

Can you describe your best boss / worst boss?

形容一下你遇過最好／最糟糕的老闆。

What do you think is the most rewarding part of being a secretary?

你認為做秘書最有意義的部分是甚麼？

What makes you passionate about this work?

是甚麼讓你對這項工作充滿熱情？

What can you tell me about our company?

你能說出有關我們公司的甚麼訊息？

Why are you leaving your current position?

你為甚麼要離開現在的職位？

What do you consider to be your core strengths?

你認為你的核心優勢是甚麼？

Chapter 12 辦公室文員／白領

「辦公室文員／白領」崗位真實演練

About the Job Seeker（求職者）	About the Interviewer（面試官）
Lorraine Chiu	Justin Cresswell
holds an Associate degree in Communication Studies（傳播學副學士學位）	HR Manager of Cornerstone Business Center
had one-year experience working as an Office Assistant（辦公室助理）	

Justin　　Hi there, I'm Justin Cresswell, the HR manager of Cornerstone Business Center. Did you find your way here OK?

Lorraine　Hello, Mr. Cresswell. My name is Lorraine. It's nice to meet you.

3-5-01

Justin　　Nice to meet you too. How are you doing today?

Lorraine　I am doing well, thanks.

Justin　　That's good. Lorraine, shall we start?

Lorraine　Yes, sure.

Justin　　Good. First of all, do you have any relevant experience working in an office?

熱門職位真實演練

Lorraine Yes. After completing my associate degree in communication studies, I worked as an **office assistant** at a **local financial firm** where I have developed my **organizational skills**, **data management skills** as well as **customer service skills**. For example, I had **to handle incoming calls** and other communications, **record information**, help organize and maintain **office common areas** and **enter information into databases**.

office assistant 辦公室助理
local financial firm 本地金融公司
organizational skills 組織能力
data management skills 數據管理技巧
customer service skills 客戶服務技巧
to handle incoming calls 處理來電
record information 記錄訊息
office common areas 辦公室公共區域
enter information into databases 將訊息輸入數據庫

Justin I see. So...what office-related software are you proficient with?

Lorraine In my previous role, I had to use **Microsoft Office** on a daily basis. I'm confident in my ability to use Word and PowerPoint and read data on an **Excel spreadsheet**. I'm also familiar with **POS system** as I had to input orders in my previous job. I used this program so often that it was second nature to me. Apart from that, I also had to help update the company website regularly. That's why I'm also familiar with **WordPress**. While some systems are different, I will **adapt** quickly since I am a fast learner.

Microsoft Office 微軟的辦公軟件套裝
Excel spreadsheet 電子試算表
POS system（Point of Sales）銷售點終端 / 銷售時點訊息系統（能夠協助處理庫存、進銷存、單據管理的系統）
WordPress 一套 Content Management System（內容管理系統）
adapt 適應

Justin	Great. So...what kind of documents do you have experience writing?
Lorraine	I have experience taking **minutes**, writing business emails, thank-you letters, **newsletters**, **annual reports** and **fax messages**.

minutes 會議記錄
newsletters 最新消息；通訊刊物
annual reports 年度報告
fax messages 傳真訊息

Justin	So have you ever encountered any difficulties in your past role as office assistant? How did you cope with it?
Lorraine	Being the office assistant at my previous company, I once **dealt** with a **frustrated** client on the phone. The client was stressed and angry because a seemingly **unwarranted charge** had been made to his credit card. Although he was shouting, I didn't **interrupt** him because I knew that he must be worried and **anxious** at that moment. After he had **thoroughly** explained the situation, I **reassure** him that I **intended to** help him in any way possible.

deal(t) with 處理
frustrated 沮喪的
unwarranted charge 不當收費
interrupt 打斷
anxious 焦慮的
thoroughly 徹底地
reassure 重新保證
intend(ed) to 有意願

Justin	Ok. Soow do you keep yourself organized when dealing with tasks and requests from multiple sources?
Lorraine	I'm a very organized person. My trick to staying organized is to keep a log of every **task**. At the beginning of each week, I have the habit of **reviewing** my calendar and **outlining** the key things I need **to accomplish**. Then, I set up

Part 1

熱門職位真實演練

reminders and **to do lists** so that I can have clear steps and time **allocated** to meet those goals. You know, nowadays, there're many great software tools that make it much easier to juggle lots of tasks. All these skills help me ensure nothing is ever forgotten.

trick 技巧
to keep a log of... 保留……的日誌
reviewing 檢查
outlining 概述
to accomplish 完成
to do lists 清單
to allocate 分配

Justin　　Great. I can feel that you are a very organized person. However, I'd like to know whether you are good at handling urgent cases? You know, sometimes things just come up suddenly.

Lorraine　Of course, not everything can be planned. When things come up last minute, like some **urgent issues**, I can **adjust** quickly and **respond** to those matters. Apart from the ability to handle urgent and immediate problems **in a proactive manner**, I'm also good at **prioritizing** tasks and do not **get overwhelmed** when working under pressure.

urgent issues 緊急問題
adjust 調整
respond 應對
in a proactive manner 積極地
prioritizing... 對……進行優先級排序
get overwhelmed 變得不知所措

Justin　　So what administrative duties do you enjoy most and least?

Lorraine　I truly enjoy working in a busy office and **solving problems on the fly**. Facing challenges makes me feel excited and **motivated**. For example, I'm very **accustomed to** working under tight deadlines. Basically, all the projects that I worked on in the previous job have **tight deadlines**.

I enjoy cooperating with colleagues to meet the requirements of our clients and to ensure that we could finish our projects **on time** successfully. Regarding the thing that I enjoy least, well....I find it stressful when things are **disorganized**. Therefore, when I see anyone needs help, I will **be more than willing to lend a helpful hand**.

solving problems on the fly 即時解決問題
motivated 有動力
accustomed to (+___ing) 習慣於 _____
tight deadlines 時間緊迫
on time 準時
disorganized 雜亂無章的
be more than willing to 樂於
to lend a helpful hand 伸出援手

Justin   Great, Lorraine. Now, I have a last question for you. What languages do you speak?

Lorraine   My **mother tongue** is Cantonese, and I speak fluent English and Mandarin.

mother tongue 母語

Justin   Good. Lorraine, is there anything you would like to ask me?

Lorraine   What would be my priorities for the first month?

Justin   If you are hired, you will have to attend a **paid training class** before you can be on the **jobsite**, which lasts for three days. After getting familiar with our company, you will begin with some **clerical duties**, including mailing and filing correspondence, **preparing payrolls**, and answering calls. Starting from the third week, you will have to help maintain accurate records, enter data, assist in **setting up new client accounts**. And you may also need to perform additional duties when required, like organizing the filing system.

paid training class 有薪培訓班
jobsite 工作現場
clerical duties 文書職責
preparing payrolls 準備工資單
setting up new client accounts 設置新的客戶帳戶

熱門職位真實演練

Lorraine	Thank you so much for providing information on this.
Justin	You're welcome, Lorraine. Do you still have any questions for me?
Lorraine	No, I think I have a pretty good understanding of the job. I believe that I can handle it **with ease**, and I hope to have the opportunity to work for you.

with ease 輕鬆地

Justin	It's been good talking to you. I can tell that you are a good candidate. Expect to hear from us within a week or so.
Lorraine	Nice meeting you too. Thank you for your time. I'm looking forward to hearing about the next steps, and don't hesitate to contact me if you have any questions or concerns in the meantime.
Justin	Sure. Thanks for coming to the interview. Goodbye.
Lorraine	Goodbye.

可能遇到的面試問題

3-5-02

🔖 Why should we hire you, and not one of many other candidates who try to get this secretary position?

你認為我們為甚麼要聘用你，而非其他申請這職位的求職者？

🔖 Describe a time when you were faced with a stressful situation.

描述一次你面對壓力的經歷。

🔖 Tell me about a time that you were not satisfied with your work performance. What did you do about it?

描述一次你對自己工作表現不滿意的經歷。你為此做了甚麼？

Describe a difficult problem you had to sort out in your previous work experience.

描述你在以前的工作經驗中必須解決的一個難題。

Can you describe your best boss / worst boss?

形容一下你遇過最好 / 最糟糕的老闆。

What can you tell me about our company?

你能說出有關我們公司的甚麼訊息？

Why are you leaving your current position?

你為甚麼要離開現在的職位？

What do you consider to be your core strengths?

你認為你的核心優勢是甚麼？

What type of duties did you handle in previous positions?

你曾負責過哪些職務？

What is your greatest strength?

你最大的優點是甚麼？

Do you have experience maintaining office equipment? If so, what type of products?

你有打理辦公設備的經驗嗎？如有的話，你負責過甚麼類型的產品？

What type of documents and formats have you generated in the past?

你過去處理過甚麼類型的文檔和檔案格式？

What are significant characteristics for a successful office assistant?

成功的辦公室助理有哪些重要特徵？

熱門職位真實演練

📌 Why do you think you're a great fit for this position?
你為甚麼認為自己非常適合這個職位？

📌 Would you be available to work extra hours if needed?
如果需要，你可以加班嗎？

📌 How do you manage confidential information?
你如何管理機密資料？

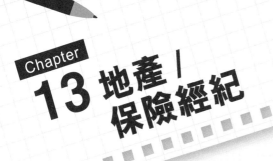

Chapter 13 地產 / 保險經紀

「地產 / 保險經紀」崗位真實演練

About the Job Seeker （求職者）	About the Interviewer （面試官）
George Au	Edmond Yeung
holds a BBA in Hospitality and Real Estate	HR Manager of Goat Property Agency Ltd.
has 1 year of relevant work experience	

Edmond　Welcome to Goat Property Agency Limited. George. I am Edmond Yeung.

George　Hello, Mr. Yeung. It's nice to meet you.

Edmond　Nice to meet you too. How are you doing today?

George　I am doing well, thanks.

Edmond　How was the traffic coming over here?

George　Well⋯ I'm so glad that the traffic was light this morning. No traffic jam and no accidents.

Edmond　That's good. George, shall we start?

George　Yes, sure.

3-6-01

熱門職位真實演練

Edmond	Okay, let me introduce myself. I'm the HR manager here and we now recruiting Real Estate Agents to cope with demand. George, I noticed that you just graduated last year. Do you have any relevant work experience?
George	Yes, after completing my BBA degree, I had worked as an Estate Agent for one year in Hong Kong.
Edmond	I see. Which company did you work for?
George	I worked for Happy Property Agency for 12 months as a junior estate agent.
Edmond	Very well, George. I'd like to know more about your experience working at Happy Property Agency. Can you describe your previous duties?
George	Sure. In my previous role, I had to **liaise with** clients **to market properties** in **the most appropriate manner** in order to maximize **the selling value**, to travel to properties and **conduct viewings**, **to handle enquiries** about properties from **potential buyers**, **to make plans** for clients, and to follow up sales and **promotional activities**. As a team member, I also needed to achieve the given sales target.

liaise with... 與……保持聯繫
to market properties 推銷物業
the most appropriate manner 最合適的方式
the selling value 銷售價值
to conduct viewings 進行觀察
to handle enquiries 處理查詢
to make plans 制定計劃
potential buyers 潛在買家
to achieve the given sales target 實現既定的銷售目標
promotional activities 促銷活動

Edmond	So, how many flats did you sell last year?
George	Last year, I sold 35 flats, including **luxury homes**, **mid-range homes**, and **starter homes**.

luxury homes 豪宅
mid-range homes 中檔住宅
starter homes「上車盤」; 起步房

（小貼士：在香港物業市場，「上車」主要形容「首次置業」。一個普通人成為業主的身份進化過程，猶如成功趕上列車的一刻，有一種身心變得安穩的感覺。）

Edmond   Then, are you familiar with this area?

George   Yes, I have experience selling in the local market to new and growing families and am very familiar with the **neighborhoods** in this area. I'm confident that I can use **my professional knowledge** to make **homebuyers** feel comfortable and confident **during their search**.

neighborhoods 鄰里

my professional knowledge 我的專業知識

homebuyers 購房者

during their search 在搜索（房屋的）過程中

Edmond   Then, do you know how to take advantage of the Internet and social media to sell homes?

George   Yes, I have experience using Facebook, Instagram and Youtube to sell properties. I'm also good at making homes look beautiful online as I have been practicing photography since high school. Last month, one of my listings got over 80 shares on Facebook and 120 comments on Instagram. What's more, in order to reach more ideal homebuyers, I also **invest** in monthly **social media ads**. This **marketing strategy** is quite **beneficial** as it has increased my sales by 10% to 15% over the past six months.

invest in 投資於

social media ads 社交媒體廣告

marketing strategy 市場策略

beneficial 有益的；有利的

Edmond   As you know, property agents always have appointments. How do you stay organized to make sure you make every appointment and won't be late?

熱門職位真實演練

George I'm a very organized person. I use multiple methods to stay organized. My trick to staying organized is **to keep a log of** every important appointment. At the beginning of each week, I have the habit of **reviewing** my calendar and **outlining** the key things I need **to accomplish**. Then, I set up reminders and **to do lists** so that I can have clear steps and time **allocated** to meet those goals. You know, nowadays, there're many great software tools that make it much easier to juggle lots of tasks. Also, I have the habit of **setting reminders** to go off half hour before I need to leave for each appointment. All these skills help me ensure nothing is ever forgotten.

trick 技巧

to keep a log of _____ 保留 xxx 的日誌

reviewing 檢查

outlining 概述

to accomplish 完成

to do lists 清單

to allocate 分配

setting reminders 設置提醒

Edmond Great. I can feel that you are a very organized person. So...what qualities make you a good real estate agent?

George I'm a good listener and I'm **detail-oriented**. Being a **conscientious** person, I always **take the extra step to** make sure my clients and potential clients are comfortable and taken care of. For examples, before **conducting viewings** with clients, I tend to **do a quick walk** by myself **in advance**. By so doing, I can **spot** details my clients may like in order to increase the chances of them liking the home.

detail-oriented 注重細節

conscientious 認真的；有責任心的

take the extra step to 做多一步；採取進一步措施

conducting viewings 進行觀察

do a quick walk 快速走走

in advance 提前；預先

spot 發現；找出

Edmond	Great, George. Now, I have a last question for you. When you meet with a client for the first time, what will you do to make sure your clients' needs are met?
George	When I meet with a client for the first time, I'll ask them some **typical** questions like their **budget, preferred location, home size, number of bedrooms** and bathrooms, and many others. This process usually takes 5 to 10 minutes, and I'll use it as a guide for our conversation. By so doing, I can **refine** their **listing options** because it helps me **to personalize** my search and select the best flats for them based on their needs.

typical 典型的
budget 預算
preferred location 首選地點
home size 房屋面積
number of bedrooms 臥室數量
refine 優化；理想化
listing options 房源選項
to personalize 個性化

Edmond	Good. George, is there anything you would like to ask me?
George	Yes. What type of career paths do people typically follow within this organization?
Edmond	In our organization, a career as a real estate agent involves you starting out on **a sales path** and **chalking up experience**. Once you have sufficient experience, you can choose between remaining just **sales focused** or **embarking on leadership and management roles**. In leadership roles, you will be engaged in **team building** and **training roles**.

a sales path 銷售道路
chalking up experience 累積經驗
sales focused 以銷售為重點
embarking on leadership and management roles 擔任領導和管理職務
team building 團隊建設
training roles 培訓角色

| George | Thank you so much for providing information on this. It sounds amazing. I'm confident that if given this opportunity, I will thrive and can contribute my selling skills and experiences to Goat Property Agency Limited. I am always **passionate** about the **Real Estate industry** and **eager** to work in a **mission-driven** company such as your company, and I'm eager to grow my **leadership skills**, **eventually** taking on **managerial responsibilities**. |

passionate 熱情的
Real Estate industry 房地產行業
eager 渴望的
mission-driven 使命導向的
leadership skills 領導能力
eventually 最終
managerial responsibilities 管理職責

Edmond	Glad to hear that you have set clear goals for yourself. Alright, George, it's been good talking to you. I can tell that you are a good candidate. Expect to hear from us within three to five days.
George	Nice meeting you too. Thank you for your time. I'm looking forward to hearing about the next steps, and don't hesitate to contact me if you have any questions or concerns in the meantime.
Edmond	Sure. Thanks for coming to the interview. Goodbye.
George	Goodbye.

可能遇到的面試問題

3-6-02

🔖 What qualities do you have that make you a great real estate agent / insurance agent?

你具備哪些素質可以使你成為出色的房地產經紀人 / 保險經紀人？

🔖 Are you able to handle rejection? If so, how?

你懂得處理被拒絕的情況嗎？如果被拒絕了怎麼辦？

What was your most successful sale?

你最成功的銷售是甚麼？

How would you differentiate yourself from your competitors?

與其他競爭對手相比，你有甚麼優勝之處？

What kind of strategy would you devise to gain clients' attention?

你有甚麼策略來吸引客戶？

As you know, it can sometimes take a few months until you sell a flat. How do you plan to motivate yourself in this sort of competitive and challenging environment?

如你所知，有時可能需要花幾個月的時間才能售出一套房子。你如何在這種充滿競爭和挑戰性的環境中激勵自己？

How do you plan to attract new clients to our company?

你打算如何吸引新客戶到我們公司？

What are your top three skills?

你最好的前三項技能是甚麼？

What skills would you like to learn and why?

你想學習甚麼技能？為甚麼？

How would your colleagues and clients describe you?

你的同事和客戶將如何形容你？

Describe a time when you worked with a demanding client looking to purchase a flat. How did you cope with the situation?

描述一次你與要求苛刻的客戶相處的經驗。你如何應付這種情況？

Describe how you would handle a demanding buyer with an inflexible budget.

你將如何應對預算不夠足而且要求多多的買家？

How do you inform potential buyers about current listings?

你如何告知潛在買家當前擁有的房源？

What has been your favorite selling experience?

你最喜歡的銷售經歷是甚麼？

What is your favorite part of working in real estate?

你最喜歡從事房地產工作的哪一部分？

Do you prefer to work independently, or as a part of a group?

你喜歡獨立工作，還是作為團隊的一部分？

Tell us about any relevant working experience you have.

告訴我任何相關的工作經驗。

What are your obligations as a Real Estate Agent?

作為房地產經紀人，你有甚麼義務？

Are you familiar with this industry?

你熟悉這個行業嗎？

面試「零售銷售員」崗位真實演練

About the Job Seeker（求職者）	About the Interviewer（面試官）
Erica Lai	Julia Greenwood
holds a BBA in Sales and Marketing	HR Manager of Louis Fashion, An international Company
has 2 years of relevant work experience	

Julia	Hi there, I'm Julia Greenwood. Welcome to Louis Fashion.
Erica	Good Morning, Miss Greenwood. I'm Erica Lai.
Julia	How was the traffic coming over here?
Erica	I'm so glad that the traffic was light this morning. No traffic jam and no accidents.
Julia	That's good. Erica, let's start the interview. Are you ready?
Erica	Yes, I am.
Julia	Great. Let me introduce myself first. I am the HR manager here. We have been interviewing applicants as we are now in need of two full-time salespeople. What do you know about Louis Fashion?

3-7-01

Appendix 2　Appendix 1

Part 2

Part 1

熱門職位真實演練

Erica　　As far as I know, Louis Fashion is an international fashion company **founded in** 1992 and **has recently expanded** its **brick-and-mortar outpost** to go online. Your company **caters to** young individuals with **a distinct sense of style**. Louis Fashion has **a vast selection of on-trend** styles, from **accessories** to **activewear** and **intimates**. I believe that **e-commerce** is **a strong fit** and an area where you have a lot of **potential for growth**. Recently, I read a news feed on your company website, and I know that **the board is eager to expand** yet still keep the personal, warm **atmosphere**. That's something I can really **appreciate**.

> founded in... 成立於 ＿＿＿＿ 年
> has recently expanded 最近擴展到
> brick-and-mortar outpost 實體店
> caters to 迎合
> a distinct sense of style 獨特的風格
> a vast selection of 多種；廣泛的選擇
> on-trend 流行的
> accessories 飾物
> activewear 運動服
> intimates 貼身內衣
> e-commerce 電子商務
> a strong fit 非常適合
> potential for growth 增長潛力
> the board 董事會
> is eager to 渴望
> expand 擴大規模
> atmosphere 氣氛
> appreciate 欣賞

Julia　　I'm glad that you've done some research before coming to here. Can you tell me what makes you a good salesperson?

Erica　　Well… First of all, I'm a hardworking salesperson who **sets foundational goals** for myself. Once I reach a **benchmark**, I **raise the bar** and continue

striving for greater heights. Secondly, I really enjoy **establishing connections** with customers and **potential customers** through **consistent** and **customized** communication. Thirdly, I'm **hyper-organized**. My calendar is full of reminders **to follow** up with customers. I have the habit of setting up **to do lists** so that I can have clear steps and time allocated to meet those goals. Plus, I always spend time with new products. This allows me to be able to answer customers' questions fluently.

sets foundational goals 設定基本目標
benchmark 基準
raise the bar 提高標準
striving for greater heights 繼續努力以達到更高目標
establishing connections 建立聯繫
potential customers 潛在客戶
consistent 持續的
customized 定制的
hyper-organized 非常有組織
to follow up 跟進
to do lists 待辦事項

Julia	So...what are your long-term career goals?
Erica	To be frank, I have some pretty **lofty** career goals. After researching your company and learning more about this position, I feel that this role fits well with my future **aspirations**. I am always **passionate** about the **retailing industry** and **eager** to work in sales in a **mission-driven** company such as Louis Fashion in which I can **elaborately comprehend** the **product market fits**, merchant characteristics, and related opportunities. I'm always looking to improve my selling skills and in particular, I'm eager to grow my **leadership skills**, **eventually** taking on **managerial responsibilities**. My career goal in the coming 5 years is to see myself promoted based on my hard work and results, eventually managing one of the branches.

熱門職位真實演練

lofty 崇高的
aspirations 志向
passionate 熱情的
retailing industry 零售業
eager 渴望的
mission-driven 使命導向的
elaborately comprehend 精心理解
product market fits 產品與市場的契合度
leadership skills 領導能力
eventually 最終
managerial responsibilities 管理職責

Julia	（小貼士：面試「銷售員」的求職者注意，你要有心理準備面試時有機會需要即時推銷一件產品。）
	(Reaches across to hand Erica the pen)
	Okay. Erica, sell me this pen now.
Erica	Okay. Let me try. (Takes a deep breath)
	When was the last time you used a pen?
Julia	An hour ago.
Erica	Do you remember what kind of pen that was?
	〔收集訊息：了解顧客上次使用筆的方式〕
Julia	No. I just grabbed a pen randomly from my desk.
Erica	Do you remember why you were using it to write?
Julia	Yea... Signing some new customer contracts.
Erica	Well, you know what? I'd like to say that signing contracts is the best use for a pen. Do you agree that signing new customer contracts is an important event for the business?
	〔強調顧客上次使用筆的重要性〕
Julia	Right.
Erica	What I mean is....here you are signing a new customer contract, an important and memorable event. All while using a very unmemorable pen...Well, look at this pen. This is the pen for important events. This is the pen you use to get deals done. When you begin using the right tool, you are in a more productive state of mind, and you begin to sign more new customer contracts.
	〔推銷出比筆更強大的東西，例如心態〕

Julia	Uh-huh.
Erica	You know what? Just this morning, I shipped more than five new boxes of these pens. (Reaches across to hand pen back to Julia) Unfortunately, this is my last pen today. Would you like to get one? Try it out. If you're not happy with it, I can come back in person to pick it up. It won't cost you a cent. What do you think? 〔再次説服顧客購買〕
Julia	Okay. I'll take this one.
Erica	Thanks, madam. Let me pack it for you.
Julia	Good job, Erica. You have good selling skills. （小貼士：記得要時刻保持謙虛。即使得到面試官的讚賞，也要保持虛心受教的態度。切忌説'Yes. I really know a lot.'之類的説話。）
Erica	Thanks, Miss Greenwood. I know that there are still many things I need to learn.
Julia	Very well, Erica. Now, I'd like to know more about your experience working as a salesperson. Can you describe your previous duties?
Erica	In my previous role as a salesperson at Joyful Boutique, I formed some significant **customer relationships**, which resulted in a **25% increase in sales** in a matter of months. Besides, I demonstrated the ability **to work under intense pressure**, sell products and services to **customers from all backgrounds**, handle customer **complaints** and solve problematic situations. I **was promoted** twice for **exceeding my sales targets** within 2 years, and I've been one of the top salespeople last year. What I am looking for now is a company that values customer relations, where I can join a strong team and have a positive impact on **customer retention** and sales.

> customer relationships 客戶關係
> a ____% increase in sales 銷售額增長了 ____%
> to work under intense pressure 在巨大的壓力下工作
> customers from all backgrounds 來自不同背景的客戶

complaints 投訴
be promoted 晉升；升職
exceeding sales targets 超出銷售目標
customer retention 客戶留存率

Julia   Great, Erica. Now, I have a last question for you. What languages do you speak?

Erica   Well, my native language is Cantonese, and I speak fluent English and Mandarin. I can speak a little Japanese.

Julia   Good. Erica, is there anything you would like to ask me?

Erica   Well, yes. I have a question. Is there any new product line recently?

Julia   Yes, our new product line is called Louis Elite. This product line will be announced within this week, which is designed to be both **trendy** and **comfy**.

trendy 時尚的
comfy 舒適的

Erica   It sounds amazing. I'm confident that if given this opportunity, I will thrive and can contribute my selling skills and experiences to Louis Fashion.

Julia   Erica, it's been good talking to you. I can tell that you are a good candidate. Expect to hear from us within a week or so.

Erica   Nice meeting you too. Thank you for your time. I'm looking forward to hearing about the next steps, and don't hesitate to contact me if you have any questions or concerns in the meantime.

Julia   Sure. Thanks for coming to the interview. Goodbye.

Erica   Goodbye.

3-7-02

Why should we hire you, and not one of the many other well-qualified applicants who try to get this position?
你認為我們為甚麼要聘用你，而非其他合格的求職者？

Have you consistently met your sales goals?
你是否一直能實現自己的銷售目標？

Are you comfortable making cold calls?
你是否適應撥打推銷電話？

Sell me this (phone / dress / pencil / other things).
向我推銷這（電話 / 衣服 / 鉛筆 / 其他東西）。

How would your colleagues describe you?
你的同事一般如何形容你？

What interests you most about this sales position?
你對該銷售職位最感興趣的是甚麼？

What makes you a good salesperson?
是甚麼讓你認為自己是一名優秀的銷售員？

Tell me about a time that you were not satisfied with your work performance. What did you do about it?
描述一次你對自己工作表現不滿意的經歷。你為此做了甚麼？

What can you tell me about our company?
你能說出有關我們公司的甚麼訊息？

Why are you leaving your current position?
你為甚麼要離開現在的職位？

What do you consider to be your core strengths?
你認為你的核心優勢是甚麼？

What type of duties did you handle in previous positions?
你曾負責過哪些職務？

What is your greatest strength?
你最大的優點是甚麼？

Why do you think you're a great fit for this position?
你為甚麼認為自己非常適合這個職位？

Would you be available to work extra hours if needed?
如果有需要，你可以加班嗎？

Appendix 1

初入
新公司

01 上班第一天

Yuki 上班的第一天

Yuki Law: 新入職同事	Charmaine Wong: HRM （人力資源經理）	Joe & Billy: 公司員工，與 Yuki 同一部門

地點：接待處（Reception）

4-1-01

Yuki	Good morning, Miss Wong. I'm so glad to meet you again. 黃小姐，早上好。很高興再次見到你。
Charmaine	Welcome aboard, Yuki. Today is your first day. Are you ready? I hope everything goes well today. Yuki，歡迎你。今天是你就職的第一天，你準備好了嗎？祝你今天一切順利。
Yuki	Thank you, Miss Wong. Yes, I'm ready. Can I meet my colleagues? 謝謝，黃小姐，我準備好了。請問可以見見我的同事嗎？
Charmaine	Sure. Come with me. Let me take you to your office. 當然可以，跟我來吧！我帶你到辦公室。
Yuki	Great. Thanks! 好的，謝謝！

Charmaine	Joe, Billy, I'd like you to meet our newcomer, Yuki. She's our new Financial Assistant. Please take care of each other from now on. Joe、Billy，來認識一下我們的新員工 Yuki，她是我們的財務助理。從現在開始，請你們互相照顧。
Billy	(shake hands) Hello, Yuki. I'm Billy, the senior Financial Analyst here. Yuki 你好。我是 Billy，這裏的高級財務分析師。
Yuki	Hello, Billy. Nice to meet you. 你好，Billy。很高興認識你。
Joe	(shake hands) I'm Joe. I'm the auditor here. 我叫 Joe。我是這裏的核數師。
Yuki	It is my pleasure to meet you! 請多指教！

4-1-02

Useful words & expressions

Welcome aboard	歡迎
Everything goes well	一切順利
Colleagues	同事
Come with me	跟我來
Newcomer	新員工；新來者
It is my pleasure to meet you.	很高興認識你；請多指教

初入新公司

■ 實踐對話

> **Yuki 上班的第二天在茶水間認識同事 Isaac**

Yuki Law: 新入職同事	Isaac: 公司員工，與 Yuki 同一部門

地點：茶水間（Pantry）

Isaac   Oh, hi, you're new here, right?
嗨，你是新來的同事，對嗎？

Yuki   Yeah, I just started yesterday. I'm a Financial Assistant.
是的，我是昨天新來的財務助理。

4-2-01

Isaac   Great. We're in the same department. You can call me Isaac.
太好了，我們屬同一個部門的，你可以叫我 Isaac。

Yuki   Hello, Isaac. Nice to meet you. I'm Yuki.
Isaac 你好，很高興認識你，我叫 Yuki。

Isaac   So how's your first day?
那……第一天上班過得怎麼樣？

Yuki   Well, it's going well overall. Although it's a little overwhelming, you know - a lot of new information to take in -I enjoy it so far.
嗯……總體來說進展也算順利。儘管一開始有一點不知所措，你也知道，作為新人需要接收的新訊息特別多，不過到目前為止我也挺享受的。

Isaac	Yea...I know that feeling. I believe you will get the hang of it.
	是的，我明白那種感覺，我相信你一定會掌握得到的。
Yuki	Thanks. I'm sure I will.
	謝謝你，我相信我可以的。
Isaac	Anyways, do let me know if you need any help. My office is over there.
	需要我幫助的話記得告訴我，我的辦公室就在那邊。
Yuki	Thank you, that's very kind of you.
	謝謝你，你真好人。
Isaac	Catch you later!
	待會見！
Yuki	See you around.
	待會兒再見。

4-2-02

Useful words & expressions

I just started yesterday/ last week/two days ago	我昨天 / 上週 / 兩天前剛入職
How's your first day	你第一天上班如何
Going well	進展順利
Overwhelming	壓迫感；不知所措；「chur」（廣東話）

初入新公司

So far/until now/Up to this point/Until now	到目前為止
Get the hang of it	掌握它
That's very kind of you	你真的是太好人了
Catch you later	待會見
See you later	稍後見（一般為幾小時到幾天，甚至更長時間）
See you soon	回頭見；我希望我能在短時間內見到你。
See you around	"Around" 帶有偶遇的含義。例如你在 office 碰見某同事，然後彼此聊了一會兒，說再見的時候就可以說："Great talking to you. See you around."
Let's grab a coffee / Let's have a coffee / Let's get a coffee	（有空）喝杯咖啡

03 向新老闆／上司介紹自己

實踐對話

Yuki 正向新老闆介紹自己

Yuki Law: 新入職同事	George Miles: 公司老闆

地點：George 的辦公室

4-3-01

Yuki	(knock on the door) （敲門）
George	Yes? Come on in. 請進來。
Yuki	Good afternoon, Mr. Miles. I'm Yuki. 邁爾斯先生中午好，我是 Yuki。
George	Oh hi, Yuki, you are new here. Right? 嗨，Yuki，你是新來的，對嗎？
Yuki	Right. I just wanted to come by and introduce myself. This is my first day here. 是的，我只是想過來自我介紹一下。今天是我在這裏工作的第一天。
George	Oh, that's great. How are you this morning? 哦，太好了。你今早過得好嗎？

Yuki	It's going well. My colleagues have been helping me learn the ropes. Mr. Miles, and you? 目前進行得順利，我的同事一直在幫助我找到工作的竅門。邁爾斯先生，那您過得好嗎？
George	Glad to hear that. I am well, too. Yuki, if you need any help, you can come to me or you can go to your general manager Edmond. Have you met him yet? 很高興聽你這樣說。我也很好。如果你需要任何幫助可以來找我，也可以去找你的總經理 Edmond。你見過他嗎？
Yuki	Yes, I met him just now. He took me out for lunch and showed me the entire office. 是的，我剛與他見面了。他帶我出去吃了頓午飯，並帶我參觀了整個辦公室。
George	Great. We work as a team here, so if you need anything, just let us know. Okay? 那就好了。我們是一個團隊來的，因此，如果你需要任何幫助，請告訴我們，好嗎？
Yuki	Sure. Thank you, sir. 當然，謝謝您，邁爾斯先生。
George	Alright. Thanks for stopping by, Yuki. Have a nice day. 好吧，感謝你順道拜訪，祝你今天過得愉快。
Yuki	Thank you so much for your time, Mr. Miles. (close the door) 邁爾斯先生，非常感謝您的寶貴時間。（關門）

4-3-02

Come by	順道
It's going well	進行得順利
Learn the ropes	找到竅門 / 線索；摸門路（*"Rope"的意思就是繩索。要成為合格的水手，首先需要學會怎樣擺弄好幾十根繩索，把船帆升上桿子，並固定在一定的位置上。當新手終於學會如何處理那一大堆 ropes 後，也就是說，after "learning the ropes"，他就能成為老手了。）
Come to me	到我這裏來
Go to your general manager	去找你的總經理
Take sb. out for lunch	帶（某人）出去吃午餐
Show sb. the entire office	帶（某人）參觀整個辦公室
Stop by	順道拜訪；短暫拜訪

初入新公司

常見的辦公室用品／文具

Ballpoint	原子筆
Bills	賬單
Binder clip / Foldback clip	裝訂夾；裝訂夾子；長尾夾
Box cutter / Cutter knife	鎅刀；剻刀；美工刀
Calculator	計算機
Calendar	日曆
Clock card machine / Punch clock	打卡機
Copier / Copy Machine	影印機
Correction fluid / White-out	塗改液
Correction tape	塗改帶
Drawer unit	抽屜格
Drawer	抽屜
Eraser	擦膠；橡皮擦
Fax machine	傳真機
File folder	文件夾；資料夾
Filing cabinet	文件櫃
Glue	膠水
Highlighter	螢光筆

Hole puncher	打孔器；打洞器
Laptop	手提電腦；筆記本電腦
Letter opener	開信刀
Magnifying	放大鏡
Marker (pen)	雙頭油筆；記號筆；馬克筆
Mic / Microphone	擴音器；麥克風；話筒
Monitor	顯示器
Paperclip	萬字夾；迴形針；曲別針
Pencil pot	筆筒
Pencil sharpener	鉛筆刨；削鉛筆機
Post-it / Sticky note	便利貼；備忘貼；便條紙
Printer	打印機
Projector	投影儀
Protractor	量角器
Ruler	直尺
Scanner	掃描機
Scissors	剪刀
Shredder	碎紙機
Speaker	揚聲器；喇叭
Stamp	印章
Stapler	釘書機
Swivel chair	轉椅
Wastebasket	廢紙簍
Webcam	網路攝像鏡頭
White board marker	白板筆
Whiteboard	白板

初入新公司

實踐對話

> Yuki 剛到公司的第一天，老闆 George Miles 正在安排其秘書 Nancy 帶她參觀公司

Yuki Law: 新入職同事	George Miles: 公司老闆	Nancy: George Miles 的秘書	Kelsey: 高級主管 & Yuki 的上司

地點：George Miles 的辦公室 & Yuki 辦公的地方

Yuki	(knock on the door) （敲門）
George	Yes? Come on in. 請進。

4-5-01

Yuki	Good afternoon, Mr. Miles. I'm Yuki. 邁爾斯先生中午好，我是 Yuki。
George	Oh hi, Yuki, you are new here. Right? 嗨，Yuki，你是新來的，對嗎？
Yuki	Right. This is my first day here. 是的，今天是我在這裏工作的第一天。
George	I'd like to take you for a tour of the office, but I'm afraid I can't because I have five meetings to attend today. I'll ask Nancy, my secretary to do that for us. Okay? 我本想帶你參觀一下辦公室的，但是恐怕不能了，因為我今天需要出席 5 個會議。因此，我會請我的秘書 Nancy 帶你參觀一下，好嗎？

Yuki	Sure. Thank you very much for your arrangement and assistance.
	當然,非常感謝您的安排和協助。
George	Nancy, would you take Miss Law for a tour of the office, please?
	Nancy, 你可以帶羅小姐參觀一下辦公室嗎?
Nancy	Yes, sir.
	是的,邁爾斯先生。
George	Thank you. Oh! Yuki, would you meet me today at 3pm for a business meeting, please?
	謝謝。對了,Yuki,你今天下午 3 時可以跟我參加商務會議嗎?
Yuki	Sure. No problem, Mr. Miles. I will be there.
	當然沒問題。邁爾斯先生,到時見。
George	Thank you!
	謝謝!
Nancy	Okay, please come with me, Miss Law.
	好,羅小姐,請跟我來。
Yuki	You can call me Yuki.
	你可以叫我 Yuki。
Nancy	Okay, Yuki. So....this will be your desk and that's your swivel chair. This is your telephone, and these are your files. The filing cabinet over there is also yours.
	好的,Yuki。這是你的辦公桌和旋轉椅。這是你的電話、文件夾。那邊的文件櫃也是你的。
Yuki	Wow!
	哇!
Nancy	Well, here are some stationery essentials for you. Here are your ballpoint, pencils, erasers, file folders, scissors, highlighters, a stapler, and a letter opener.
	這裏有一些文具用品是給你的。這是你的原子筆、鉛筆、橡皮擦、文件夾、剪刀、螢光筆、釘書機和開信刀。
Yuki	Thank you so much.
	太感謝了。
Nancy	You're welcome.
	別客氣。

初入新公司

Yuki	Right, nice to meet you, Nancy. Do you work here every day? 對了 Nancy，很高興認識你。你每天都回來上班嗎？
Nancy	Yes. I work here Monday to Saturday. How about you? 是的。我星期一至星期六也會在。你呢？
Yuki	Me too, I'm free on Sundays. 我也是，我星期日放假的。
Nancy	So....if you have some free time, maybe we could grab a coffee? 那如果你有空閒時間，也許我們可以喝杯咖啡？
Yuki	Sure! That will be great. 當然！那挺棒的。
Nancy	Oh right, if you need to send a fax, the fax machine is over there. 哦，對了，如果你需要發送傳真的話，傳真機就在那邊。
Yuki	Thanks. And what about computer? 謝謝。那電腦呢？
Nancy	Your computer is over there. 你的電腦在那邊。
Yuki	Okay. Thanks. 好的，謝謝。
Nancy	Oh, Yuki. I'd like to introduce you to Kelsey, the Senior Supervisor. 對了 Yuki，我想向你介紹我們的高級主管 Kelsey。
Yuki	It's nice to meet both of you. 很高興認識您們倆。
Kelsey	It's nice to meet you too. Yuki, today is your first day, right? 很高興認識你。Yuki，今天是你第一天上班，對嗎？
Yuki	Yes. 是的。
Kelsey	Welcome to our company. In fact, we're in the same team and I'll be your supervisor. Nancy, do you mind if I take Yuki now and talk to her about her new job?

歡迎來到我們的公司。實際上，我們是同一個團隊的，我是你的主管。Nancy，你介意我現在帶 Yuki 去我的辦公室和她談談她的新工作嗎？

Nancy　Not at all. I just finished giving her the company tour. Well, see you around, Yuki.
沒問題。我剛剛帶她參觀了公司。好吧，Yuki，晚點見。

Yuki　See you later, Nancy.
Nancy 待會兒見。

4-5-02

初入新公司

Useful words & expressions

Come on in	請進
To take you for a tour of the office	帶你參觀辦公室
Secretary	秘書
Arrangement	安排
Assistance	協助
A tour of the office	參觀辦公室
Please come with me	請跟我來
Swivel chair	旋轉椅
Filing cabinet	文件櫃
Stationery essentials	文具用品
Senior Supervisor	高級主管
Company tour	參觀公司

06 員工培訓

一般來說，一些比較有規模的公司也會為新入職的新人安排新人訓練（new employee orientation；NEO），藉以幫助他們盡快了解工作內容及作業流程。新人訓練的英文為 new employee orientation，常縮寫表示為 NEO。

以與「員工培訓」相關的詞彙／短語

A comprehensive training system	全面的培訓系統
A series of training seminars	一系列的培訓研討會
As part of the induction flow	作為入職流程的一部分
Company culture	公司文化
Department training	部門培訓
Employee manual	員工手冊
Employee onboarding	員工入職
Employee training	員工培訓
English training	英語訓練

Equal opportunities for career development and promotion	平等的職業發展和晉升機會
Financial support for training programmes	培訓計劃的資金支持
Further study	進修
Job-related training	與工作有關的培訓
Job-specific training	特定崗位的培訓
Learning objectives/goals	學習目標
Management practices	管理實務
Mission	使命
New employee orientation / New Hire Orientation	新員工入職培訓
New hires/New recruits	新入職員工
New staff induction flow	新員工入職流程
On a continuing basis	持續地
On-duty training	在職培訓
Orientation program	定向課程；新人訓練
Overseas and local employees	海外和本地員工
Personnel training	人才培養；員工培訓
Post-orientation training	入職後培訓
Potential employees	潛在員工

初入新公司

Regular training for employees	對員工進行定期培訓
Support center	支援中心
The company's code of conduct	公司的行為準則
The enrollment process	入職手續
The personnel department	人事部門
To arrange physical check	安排體檢
To attend external vocational training	參加外部職業培訓
To carry out inspection	進行檢查
To conduct new employee orientation training	進行新員工入職培訓
To go through a strict process	通過嚴格的正規流程
To input information	輸入信息
To learn the structure of the _____ position	了解 _____ 職位的結構
To promise to obey _____	承諾遵守 _____
Training course on corporate secretaries and staff	公司秘書和員工培訓課程
Training materials	培訓教材
Training modules	培訓課程
Vocational skills	職業技能

辭職
相關事項

很少人會在同一間公司裏工作一輩子，離職的原因有許多，有些人會因為對公司或待遇感到不滿意而決定離開；有些人會因為尋覓更好的工作前景而放棄現職；亦有些人單純為了換換新的工作環境而選擇轉工。求職並不是一件容易事，可能需要「過五關斬六將」，施盡渾身解數才取得一席之位。可是你又知道嗎？求職難，離職亦同樣艱難！

不論你是基於甚麼原因而離職都必須按照既定的慣例，提早按程序向公司遞交離職申請。提交辭職信後就等於完成離職手續了嗎？不，你還得取得公司的批准，離職申請才可生效。你要有心理準備，整個離職申請的流程並不會如你預期中那麼順暢，過程中也許會遇到許多不同阻滯或小插曲。

如果你是打算辭去原本的工作在另一間公司尋找新的工作，你有可能需要於在職期間請假去面試，如果遇到這種情況，該如何向公司開口呢？

當你已經為未來鋪好路，下定決心要辭退現職工作的時候，又該如何撰寫一封大方得體的辭職信呢？

當你咬緊牙關、克服尷尬，將求職信遞交給僱主或上司後，如果對方挽留你又該如何應對呢？面對挽留的時候，如果想和對方談條件又該怎樣跟對方交涉？如果你最終決定堅持原有的計劃，選擇堅決辭職，又該如何拒絕對方的挽留呢？

正所謂「山水有相逢」，大家緊記在離職一事上處理得體合宜，因為也許他日你會再次與對方「交手」，可能是在其他場合相遇，又可能將來有求於對方，需要請求對方替你寫推薦信（reference letter）。

總而言之，辭職也要顧及體面，要「好聚好散」，就算選擇離去也切記要給舊僱主留下一個好印象。

辭職相關事項

01 在職期間如何請假去面試

大部分公司都會安排在 office hours（辦公時間）內進行面試。因此，如果你本身有正職，請假面試的確是一件相當傷腦筋的事。假如你同時收到多個面試通知的話，你可以盡量嘗試把所有面試安排在同一天，以避免不斷請假，讓現職公司發現你有強烈的離職意欲。你也可以善用 annual leave（年假），按正常程序申請年假去面試。

假如現職公司實在難以讓你請假，筆者建議你別一下子投寄大量求職信，而是看到心儀且合適的工作時才「出擊」，以免因漁翁撒網導致自己隔天便請一次假驚動全公司。

倘若你沒有年假，又必須請 personal leave（事假）面試，記得撰寫一封正式的請假電郵，交待清楚請假時間（盡量少於兩天）、目前工作內容 / 進度 / 職務代理人 / 代班人等，以表示自己是一個有責任感的員工。同時，記得預早安排好工作，減少讓同事「執手尾（處理別人遺留下來的麻煩事）」。

■ 表達「請假」的必學句型

I would like to take a personal day off from work on _____(date).

我希望於 _____（日期）放事假一天。

I would like to take a day off because _____.

我想請假一天，因為我 _____。

I'd like to take official leave of absence for ____ day(s).

我要請 ____ 天的年假。

I would like to request a leave of absence because_____.

我懇請公司批准本人因 _____ 告假。

I would like to ask for a one-day/two-day leave to _____.

我想請一 / 兩天假來 _____。

辭職相關事項

「請假」電郵範例

To: Charmaine Fong [charmainefong@email.com]
From: Zephyr Yeung [zephyryeung@email.com]
Subject: **Upcoming Leave of Absence**

Dear Miss. Fong,

〔交待請假日期、時間〕This is Zephyr, a junior marketing assistant working in your company. I would like to take a personal day off from work on Friday, May 1.

〔交待目前工作、職務代理人〕I am currently working on the ABC project, and Edmond will be stepping in **to handle my responsibilities**（處理我的職責）while I am away. In addition, I've talked to the other members of my team, and they are also ready to **^step up to the plate** during my absence.

〔緊急聯絡方式〕I will complete all my **pending**（待處理的）work after I come back and in case of any urgent work, you can contact me on my personal number as well.

〔感謝對方的考慮和批准〕**I appreciate your consideration and approval to my request**（感謝您的考慮和批准）. Thank you so much.

Yours sincerely,
Zephyr Yeung

^Step up to the plate（着手開始某項工作）
=start to handle
=help
(Plate = 本壘板。當一名棒球員要擊球時，他需要先踏上本壘。因此，step up to the plate 意指着手開始某項工作。)

02 撰寫辭職信

辭職也要顧及體面，要「好聚好散」，就算選擇離去也切記要給舊僱主留下一個好印象。以下，筆者為大家整合了辭職信必須包含的元素和一些注意事項，讓你可以輕鬆學會寫一封得體的辭職信。

撰寫辭職信的元素如下：

第一步	在離職信開首交代職位、離職日期
第二步	交待離職原因
第三步	禮貌地答謝公司這段期間的栽培
第四步	交代交接安排
第五步	大方向公司送上祝福

辭職相關事項

2.1 交代職位、離職日期

Formal notification (n phr.)	正式通知
To resign (v.)	辭職
Resignation (n.)	辭職
Last day (n phr.)	最後上班日
Effective two weeks/one month from this notification (phr.)	從本通知起兩週／一個月生效

實用句式 1

Please accept this letter as formal notification that I am resigning from my position as _____ (position) with _____ (company's name). My last day will be _____ (last working date).

請接受此函為辭職的正式通知，以辭去我在 _____（公司名稱）公司 _____（職位）的職務，*最後上班日期為 _____（最後上班日期）。

*一般來說，離職需要提早 2 星期至 1 個月通知，記得留意公司的政策。

例句

Please accept this letter as formal notification that I am resigning from my position as junior marketing assistant with Advertising Expert. My last day will be 10 May 2021, one month from now.

請接受此函為辭職的正式通知，以辭去我在 Advertising Expert 初級市場助理的職務，最後上班日期為 2021 年 5 月 10 日，即 1 個月後。

實用句式 2

Please accept this letter as formal notification of my resignation from my position as _____ (position) at _____ (company's name). My last day will be _____(last working date).

請接受這封信，作為我辭職的正式通知，以辭去 _____（公司名稱）公司的 _____（職位）的職務。我的最後上班日期為 _____（最後上班日期）。

例句

Please accept this letter as formal notification of my resignation from my position as Junior Sales Representative at L&Y Collection Ltd. My last day will be 10 May 2021, three weeks from now.

請接受這封信，作為我辭職的正式通知，以辭去 L & Y Collection Ltd 初級銷售代表的職務。我的最後上班日期為 2021 年 5 月 10 日，即 3 星期後。

The purpose of this letter is to announce my resignation from_____ (company's name) as _____ (position), effective one month from this notification, _____(last working date).

這封信的目的是宣佈我從 _____ （公司名稱）公司辭去 _____ （職位）的職務，自本通知之日起 1 個月後生效，即 _____ （最後上班日期）。

例句

The purpose of this letter is to announce my resignation from L&Y Collection Ltd. as Junior Sales, effective one month from this notification, 28 May 2021.

這封信的目的是宣佈我從 L&Y Collection Ltd. 公司辭去初級銷售代表的職務，自本通知之日起 1 個月後生效，即 2021 年 5 月 28 日。

2.2 交代離職原因

Useful words/expressions

After much consideration/ deliberation (prep phr.)	經過深思熟慮
To move on to new challenges (v phr.)	迎接新挑戰

Opportunity (n.)	機會
To accept a new position (v phr.)	接受新職位
New direction of my career (n phr.)	我的職業發展新方向
To grow professionally (v phr.)	專業地發展
To relocate (v.)	搬遷
Family circumstances (n phr.)	家庭情況

實用句式

1. After much consideration, I feel it is time to move on to new challenges, and I will be working for _____.

   經過深思熟慮，我認為現在是應對新挑戰的時候了，我將在 _____ 工作。

2. I have accepted a position as _____ (position). This opportunity gives me the chance to _____.

   我已接受一個新的職位，以擔任 _____（職位）一職。這將為我提供 _____。

3. After much deliberation, I've decided to accept a new position that will _____.

   經過深思熟慮，我決定接受一個新的職位，這將 _____。

4. I am writing to inform you that I have no choice but to resign from my role as _____ (position) at your company.

來函僅通知您，在別無選擇下，我只能辭去　貴公司 _____（職位）一職。

離職常見原因（一）：轉工

參考例句

After much consideration, I feel it is time to move on to new challenges, and I will be working for a local non-profit organization. I am looking forward to the new direction of my career, even though I will miss my work with you.

經過深思熟慮，我認為現在是應對新挑戰的時候了，我將在本地的一家非營利組織工作。儘管我會想念與您一起工作的日子，但我仍期待着職業發展的新方向。

After much deliberation, I've decided to accept a new position that will provide an opportunity to grow professionally.

經過深思熟慮，我決定接受一個新的職位，這將為我提供一個專業發展的機會。

📌 I have accepted a position as sales representative. This opportunity gives me the chance to grow professionally and will allow me to relocate just a few kilometers from my family.

我已接受一個新的職位，以擔任銷售代表一職。這將為我提供一個專業發展的機會。此外，我也能搬到離家人僅幾公里以外的地方。

離職常見原因（二）：工作地點

■ 參考例句

📌 I was recently offered a new opportunity with a company headquartered very close to my home and have decided to take their offer.

最近，一家總部位於我家附近的公司為我提供了新的就業機會，因此，我決定接受這份工作。

📌 I have accepted a new position as receptionist. This opportunity will allow me to relocate just a few kilometers from my family.

我已接受一個新的職位，以擔任接待員一職。這個機會將使我能夠搬到離家人僅幾公里以外的地方。

辭職相關事項

■ 參考例句

📌 I am writing to inform you that I have no choice but to resign from my role as clerk at your company. Family circumstances require my full attention at this time and leave me unable to continue in this role.

來函僅通知您，在別無選擇下，我只能辭去　貴公司文員一職，因為目前的家庭情況，我需全心全意照顧家庭，因而無法繼續擔任這職務。

2.3　答謝公司的栽培

Useful words/expressions

Be not an easy decision (v phr.)	絕非一個容易的決定；絕非易事
Professional development (n phr.)	專業的發展
Personal development (n phr.)	個人發展
The industry (n.)	該行業
My fellow employees (n phr.)	我的同事們

求職英語一本通

Thank you for the support and the opportunities you have provided me in _____. You and your team have created a climate that _____ , and I will definitely miss you all.

感謝您在過去 _____（在該公司上班的年資）年中為我提供的支持和機會。您和您的團隊也營造了一種 _____ 的氛圍，我一定會想念您們的。

例句

Thank you for the support and the opportunities you have provided me in these two years. You and your team have created a climate that makes it a pleasure to come to work each day, and I will definitely miss you all.

感謝您在過去 2 年為我提供的支持和機會。您和您的團隊也營造了一種讓我每天上班都感到高興的氛圍，我一定會想念您們的。

Appendix 2

Appendix 1

Part 2

Part 1

辭職相關事項

This was not an easy decision to make on my part. The past _____ have been very rewarding. I've _____ .Thank you for the professional and personal development you have assisted me with over the last _____ years.

就我而言，這絕非一個容易的決定。在過去的 _____ （在該公司上班的年資）年中，我獲益良多。我 _____ _____（簡單描述過往在公司的經歷）。 感謝您在過去 _____ 年為我提供的專業和個人發展。

例句

This was not an easy decision to make on my part. The past two years have been very rewarding. I've enjoyed working for you, observing how our production operations have expanded, and managing a very successful team dedicated to a quality manufactured product delivered on time. Thank you for the professional and personal development you have assisted me with over the last two years.

就我而言，這絕非一個容易的決定。在過去的 2 年 中，我獲益良多。我很高興能為公司服務，一起觀察 我們的生產運營擴展、一起管理一支非常成功的團 隊、一起致力於準時交付高質量的製成品。感謝您在 過去 2 年為我提供的專業和個人發展。

I would like to thank you for all of the great opportunities you have given me as an employee at _____ (company's name). I have learned so much about the _____ industry from working with my fellow employees and supervisors.

我要感謝您過去為我這個 _____（公司名稱）公司員工帶來所有珍貴的機會。通過與同事和主管合作，我學會了很多 _____ 行業的東西。

例句

I would like to thank you for all of the great opportunities you have given me as an employee at 3+3 Fashion. I have learned so much about the fashion industry from working with my fellow employees and supervisors.

我要感謝您過去為我這個 3 + 3 時裝員工帶來所有珍貴的機會。通過與同事和主管合作，我學會了很多時裝行業的東西。

Useful words/expressions

Transition (n.)	交接期間 / 過渡期間
Replacement (n.)	替代（者）
Successor (n.)	接替人
To find and train my replacement (v phr.)	尋找並訓練我的接替人 / 替代者
To hope our paths cross again (v phr.)	希望我們於未來有機會再次合作
Assistance (n.)	幫助
To facilitate the seamless passing of my responsibilities to _____ (v phr.)	為了使我的職責無縫地傳遞給 _____

🔖 If I can be of any assistance during this transition in order to facilitate the seamless passing of my responsibilities to my successor, please let me know.

如果在此過渡期間我能為您提供任何幫助，以便我將職責無縫地傳遞給我的接替人，請告訴我。

🔖 I would be glad to help however I can. I wish you and L & Y LTD. continued success, and I do hope to stay in touch with you in the future.

我很樂意為您提供任何幫助的。在此，我祝願您和 L & Y LTD 一直保持成功。希望我們能一直保持聯繫。

🔖 If I can do anything to help with your transition in finding and training my replacement, please let me know.

請告訴我如何可以在過渡期提供援助，如需要我幫忙尋找和培訓下一位接替人，煩請告知。

🔖 I wish you and the company all the best. I do hope our paths cross again in the future.

祝願您和公司一切順利，希望我們於未來有機會再次合作。

🔖 Please let me know if I can help in any way to assist you in hiring and/or training my replacement before my departure.

請告知我是否需要在離職前幫助您找尋或 / 和培訓我下一位接替人。

Appendix 2

Appendix 1

Part 2

Part 1

辭職相關事項

離職信範例

Dear Mr. Lau,

Please accept this letter as **formal notification**（正式通知）of my resignation from my position as Marketing Assistant at L&Y Ltd. My last day will be 10 May 2021, three weeks from now.

After **much consideration**（深思熟慮），I feel it is time to move on to new challenges, and I will be working for a local non-profit organization. I am looking forward to **the new direction of my career**（職業發展的新方向），even though I will miss my work with you.

This was not **an easy decision**（容易的決定）to make on my part. The past two years have been very rewarding. I've enjoyed working for you, observing how our production operations have expanded. Thank you for the professional and personal development you have assisted me with over the last two years. I have learned so much about the fashion industry from working with my fellow employees and supervisors.

If I can be **of any assistance**（提供任何幫助）during this **transition**（過渡期）in order to facilitate **the seamless passing**（無縫的傳遞）of my responsibilities to my successor, please let me know. I will do everything possible to wrap up my duties and train other team members.

I wish the company continued success, and I hope **to stay in touch**（保持聯繫）in the future.

Yours sincerely,
Elizabeth Choi

03 被公司挽留應該如何應對？

3.1 如何爭取加薪？

假如你提出辭職後，老闆決定加薪挽留，你該用甚麼態度應對？假如你純粹因為薪酬待遇不如理想，而非其他因素而決定離開的話，的確可以嘗試爭取「加人工（加薪）」。

在請求加薪前，記得先準備好具體資料，證明你的辦事效率及對公司的貢獻，並調查類似職務的人目前的薪資狀況。準備愈周全，待遇就可能更優越。

與公司討論薪金待遇時，不妨多從自己對公司的貢獻着手，陳述自己的工作表現、業績、工作年資等，強調自己的價值，務求獲得公司的認同並進而以取得加薪的機會。

辭職相關事項

Annual expenditure (n phr.)	年度支出
Annual salary (n phr.)	年薪
Basic/base salary (n phr.)	基本工資 / 底薪
Commitment (n.)	承諾；責任
Comparable jobs (n phr.)	相類職位
Dedication (n.)	貢獻
Doesn't meet my expectations (v phr.)	不符合我的期望
Fair wage (n phr.)	合理工資
Get a raise (n phr.)	加薪
Implement cost-effective solutions (v phr.)	實施符合成本效益的解決方案
Market price (n phr.)	市場價
Minimum wage (n phr.)	最低工資
Monthly salary (n phr.)	月薪
Presentable (adj.)	令人滿意的；像樣的
Qualification (n.)	資格
Retention rate of my clients (n phr.)	我的客戶的保留率

Starting salary (n phr.)	起薪點
Take on extra responsibilities (n phr.)	承擔額外的責任
Take on extra work (n phr.)	承擔了額外的工作
The go-to person (n phr.)	大家的求助對象

2-3.1-02

實用句式

1. During the past _____ years in this company, I took on extra work and responsibilities because I know that my performance is closely tied to the team's performance.

在這裏工作的 ___ 年中，我承擔了額外的工作和更多的責任，因為我知道我的表現與團隊績效是唇齒相依的。

2. Since I _____ , our customer base has grown by ____ percent.

自從我 _____ 後，公司的客戶已增長百分之 ___。

Appendix 2

Appendix 1

Part 2

Part 1

辭職相關事項

319

3. Though I enjoy working here, and I appreciate any opportunity the company offers me, I regret to tell you that my current salary doesn't meet my expectations.

雖然我很喜歡在這裏工作，也非常感謝公司為我提供的機會，但我很遺憾的告訴您，目前的薪資並不符合我的期望。

4. I would like to ask for a ___ percent raise, based on the excellent customer feedback I frequently receive.

鑑於我經常收到非常好的客戶反饋，我想要求加薪百分之 ___。

模擬情境

2-3.1-03

情景：老闆 Oscar 找 Jacky 談談工資。

Oscar	Jacky, I received your resignation letter yesterday. May I know, what's the main reason? Is it because of salary?
	Jacky，我昨天收到了你的辭職信。我可以知道主要原因嗎？是因為薪金問題嗎？
Jacky	To be frank, I really enjoy working here, and I appreciate any opportunity the company offers me, but I regret to tell you that my current salary doesn't meet my expectations.

坦白説，我真的很喜歡在這裏工作，也非常感謝公司為我提供的機會，但是很遺憾地告訴您，我目前的工資沒有達到我的期望。

Oscar   I see. What are your expectations, based on your performance?

那麼，根據你的表現，你的期望是甚麼？

Jacky   During the past 4 years in this company, I've been taking on extra work and responsibilities because I know that my performance is closely tied to the team's performance.

在這裏工作的 4 年中，我承擔了額外的工作和更多的責任，因為我知道我的表現與團隊績效是唇齒相依的。

Oscar   Go on.

請繼續説。

Jacky   Also, after I redesigned our website last year, our customer base has grown by 25%. I've also saved annual expenditure by 10% for our company. I believe I've gone above and beyond the benchmarks we set for my position when I arrived at the company 4 years ago. However, my salary has remained the same since March 2018. From my research, I've learned that 5% is a reasonable increase and in line with what I've contributed.

另外，自去年我重新設計了公司的網站之後，我們的客戶群增長了 25%。我還為公司節省了 10% 的年度開支。我相信已經超越了 4 年前剛進入公司時定下的基準了。但是，自 2018 年 3 月以來，我的工資卻一直維持不變。我做了相關的研究，並了解到 5% 是合理的增長，與我的貢獻相符。

Oscar   Well, I agree that you've definitely applied yourself, and the company's bottom line is much better now. I will get back to you tomorrow. What do you think?

嗯，我同意你的確非常努力，而公司的盈虧狀況也因此更好。我明天會答覆你。

Jacky   Sure. I appreciate you giving it some thought.

好的，謝謝您願意考慮（我的情況）。

辭職相關事項

1 記得保持理性討論，千萬別以辭職作為要求「加人工（加薪）」的威脅或「最後通牒」。因為即使最終成功爭取，僱主仍然會記得你當初決定離開的態度，這樣的話，即使將來表現再好，亦難以得到上司的歡心。

錯誤示範

If you don't give me a raise, I'm out of here.
如果你不給我加薪，我便會離職。

2 遞辭職信前要先三思。如果你純粹因為薪酬待遇不如理想而決定離開，建議請先與上司或老闆討論，絕不要以辭職要脅加薪。

3.2 如何拒絕公司的挽留？

假如你提出辭職後，老闆決定加薪挽留，你該用甚麼態度應對？假如你並非因為薪酬待遇不如理想決定離開，而是因為其他因素（如：已經找到新工作、家庭原因、私人原因），你可以有禮貌地告知對方去意已決，並答謝公司這段日子的照顧，然後大方向公司送上祝福。

總而言之，辭職也要顧及體面，要「好聚好散」，就算選擇離去也切記要給舊僱主留下一個好印象。

模擬情境

情景：老闆 Oscar 嘗試挽留 Jacky，但 Jacky 去意已決。

2-3.2-01

Oscar	Jacky, I received your resignation letter yesterday. May I know the main reason? Is it because of salary? Jacky，我昨天收到了你的辭職信。我可以知道主要原因嗎？是因為薪金問題嗎？
Jacky	To be frank, I really enjoy working here, and I appreciate any opportunity the company offers me, but after much consideration, I feel it is time to move on to new challenges, and I will be working for a local non-profit organization. I am looking forward to the new direction of my career, and I will definitely miss my work with you. 坦白說，我真的很喜歡在這公司工作，也很感激公司為我提供的機會，但是經過深思熟慮後，我覺得現在是面對新挑戰的時候了，我將在本地的一家非營利組織工作。我期待着職業發展的新方向，並會懷念與您一起工作的時光。
Oscar	I see. I'm glad to hear that you've figured out your new career goals. However, if we arrange you for other more challenging positions, will you consider staying here? 明白，得知你已經確定了新的職業目標，我也替你感到非常高興。但是，如果我們安排你擔任其他更具挑戰性的職位，你會考慮留在這裏嗎？
Jacky	Thank you for your appreciation. However, I'm sorry to tell you that I've already decided to move on. Indeed, this was not an easy decision to make on my part. The past 2 years have been very rewarding. I've enjoyed working for you, observing how our production operations have expanded, and managing a very successful team dedicated

辭職相關事項

to a quality manufactured product delivered on time. Thank you for the professional and personal development you have assisted me with over the last 2 years.

感謝您對我的賞識。但是很抱歉告訴您，我去意已決了。說真的，就我而言，這不是一個容易的決定。在過去的 2 年中，我獲益良多。我很高興能為公司服務、一起觀察生產運營擴展、一起管理一支非常成功的團隊、一起致力於準時交付高質量的製成品。感謝您在過去 2 年為我提供的專業和個人發展。

Oscar Alright. Jacky, thank you for everything you have done for our company in the past 2 years. Let's keep in touch. Best of luck to you in your new job.

好吧。Jacky，謝謝你在過去 2 年為我們公司所做的一切，我們保持聯繫吧。祝你在新工作中一切順利！

Jacky Thank you. I wish you and the company all the best. I do hope our paths cross again in the future. If I can do anything to help with your transition in finding and training my replacement, please let me know.

謝謝您。我也祝願您和公司一切順利，希望我們於未來有機會再次合作。請告訴我如何可以在過渡期提供援助，如需要我幫忙尋找和培訓下一位接替人，煩請告知。

Oscar Sure. Thanks, Jacky.

好的，謝謝，Jacky。

04 最後上班日（Last day）注意事項

在離職前的最後一天，工作內容應該和平日有所不同，我們需要處理許多工作交接等事項。以下，筆者將列出有甚麼事情需要在 last day 處理。建議大家做好最後一棒的交接工作，給自己、給公司劃上一個完美的句號。

一：工作交接

一般來説，員工離職前需要填寫一份交接表格。如果沒有也可以根據自己的交接內容制定一個交接表，清楚列明你要交接的工作、重要資料存放的地方等，以避免在你離職後公司又拿各種工作的問題找你麻煩。

二：清理工作空間和電腦內的資料

離開前，記得認真清理桌面和電腦，把不重要的文件以及私人文件刪除，並記得解除電腦私人密碼的密碼設置。假如你有一些涉及敏感訊息的資料文件，最好用碎紙機銷毀文件，以免新人來整理你遺留的文件時看到不該看的資料，令你有可能會因洩露公司機密而被公司起訴。

辭職相關事項

325

三：去人事部和財務部辦理離職手續

一般來説，人事部和財務部是每個離職員工臨離開前都要去的部門，以處理「離職證明」、「合同解除」、「財務報銷」、「工資確認」及「查詢強積金安排」等事宜。

四：派發「散水餅」

在廣東話中，「散水」的意思是「離開、解散」。顧名思義，「散水餅」就是 Last Day 自掏腰包買給一起艱苦奮鬥的同事們的糕點。買散水餅的意義就是向同事表達感謝之情。

離開前，你也可以視乎情況，發送一封臨別電郵給同事，順便感謝他們這段日子的照顧，並告訴他們保持聯絡。

臨別電郵範例

Dear all,

As you already know, I'll be leaving my position as Sales Representative here at Brilliant Star, and today is my last day.

While I'm excited about the new opportunity, there's also a big part of me that's sad to be saying goodbye to amazing colleagues just like you. I can't tell you how much I've enjoyed our time working together, and how much I value the friendship you've shown me over the past two years.

This might be the end of my time with Brilliant Star, but it's definitely not the end of our friendship. You have my contact number - so don't hesitate to reach out when you want to grab coffee or lunch, and I'll be sure to do the same!

It's been great working together, and I'll definitely keep in touch!

All the best,
Amber Choi

適合各行各業的面試實戰指南

著者
Zephyr Yeung

責任編輯
周宛媚

裝幀設計
鍾啟善

排版
何秋雲、辛紅梅、楊詠雯

出版者
萬里機構出版有限公司
香港北角英皇道499號北角工業大廈20樓
電話：2564 7511　　傳真：2565 5539
電郵：info@wanlibk.com
網址：http://www.wanlibk.com
　　　http://www.facebook.com/wanlibk

發行者
香港聯合書刊物流有限公司
香港荃灣德士古道 220-248 號荃灣工業中心 16 樓
電話：2150 2100　　傳真：2407 3062
電郵：info@suplogistics.com.hk

承印者
美雅印刷製本有限公司
香港觀塘榮業街 6 號海濱工業大廈 4 樓 A 室

出版日期
二○二一年五月第一次印刷

規格
大 32 開（210 mm × 142 mm）